The Viking Symbol Mystery

Other Armada Adventure Stories by Franklin W. Dixon

The Mystery of the Aztec Warrior
The Arctic Patrol Mystery
The Haunted Fort
The Mystery of the Whale Tattoo
The Mystery of the Disappearing Floor
The Mystery of the Desert Giant
The Mystery of the Melted Coins
The Mystery of the Spiral Bridge
The Clue of the Screeching Owl
While the Clock Ticked
The Twisted Claw
The Wailing Siren Mystery
The Secret of the Caves
The Secret of Pirates' Hill
The Flickering Torch Mystery
The Secret of the Old Mill
The Shore Road Mystery
The Great Airport Mystery
The Sign of the Crooked Arrow
The Clue in the Embers
What Happened at Midnight
The Sinister Signpost
Footprints Under the Window
The Crisscross Shadow
Hunting for Hidden Gold
The Mystery of Cabin Island
The Mark on the Door
The Yellow Feather Mystery
The Hooded Hawk Mystery
The Secret Agent on Flight 101
The Tower Treasure
The Mystery of the Missing Friends
The Mystery of the Chinese Junk
Night of the Werewolf
The Mystery of the Samurai Sword
The Pentagon Spy
The Apeman's Secret
The Mummy Case
The Mystery of Smugglers Cove
The Stone Idol
The Vanishing Thieves
The Outlaw's Silver
The Submarine Caper
The Four-Headed Dragon
The Infinity Clue
Track of the Zombie

The Hardy Boys® Mystery Stories

The Viking Symbol Mystery

Franklin W. Dixon

Armada

First published in the U.K. in 1974 by
William Collins Sons & Co. Ltd., London and Glasgow.
First published in Armada in 1983 by
Fontana Paperbacks,
8 Grafton Street, London W1X 3LA.
This impression 1983

Printed and bound in Great Britain by
William Collins Sons & Co. Ltd., Glasgow.

CONTENTS

CHAPTER		PAGE
1	RADIO THREAT	9
2	A MYSTERIOUS LABEL	17
3	RUNE STONE CURSE	26
4	DANGEROUS SOLO	33
5	DETECTIVE'S DOUBLE	41
6	CANADIAN GIANT	49
7	WHITE WATER	55
8	MISSING CAMPERS	64
9	GRIZZLY CHARGE	73
10	AN AMAZING SUSPECT	80
11	SURPRISE TACTICS	89
12	OFFBEAT ASSIGNMENT	99
13	EXPLOSION	107
14	BUFFALO PARK CLUE	114
15	THE GREY TERROR	120
16	SECRET INGREDIENT	126
17	VIKING MESSAGE	132
18	WHISTLER'S SIGNAL	139
19	STAMPEDE!	145
20	NORSEMEN'S TREASURE	150

The rock-like fist cracked against Frank's jaw.

·1·

Radio Threat

"DAD, why did you want us here for a meeting tonight?" asked blond, seventeen-year-old Joe Hardy.

"Is it about one of your new cases?" The speaker was Joe's tall, dark-haired, eighteen-year-old brother, Frank.

"Yes. I want you five boys to hear a radio report from Sam Radley," Fenton Hardy replied. "Frank, warm up the two-way short-wave radio." The tall, well-built private investigator glanced at his watch. "It's almost nine. Sam will be broadcasting any second."

The other boys in the room were the Hardys' pals— stout, easygoing Chet Morton, lanky Biff Hooper, and bright-eyed Tony Prito. The boys exchanged excited glance.s A message from Radley, Mr Hardy's partner, meant mystery!

Just then a crackling sound came from the radio receiver and a voice spoke over the air waves: "Radley reporting. Investigation proceeding as planned. Latest episode is stolen float plane. Owned by guest . . ." Suddenly the voice faded.

"The signal's being jammed!" Mr Hardy exclaimed, grasping the tuning knob and trying to clear the

9

jumble of static. "Someone else must be using our wave length."

As suddenly as it had started, the crackling disappeared. Then a strange, deep voice said:

"*Stay away, Hardy!*"

"That's not Sam!" Joe exclaimed, and the others stared in astonishment.

"*S-s-sh!*" Frank leaped up and bent over the set.

The new voice continued: "*Hardy, stay away! You'll never get out of the Northwest Territories alive!*"

The intruder became silent. There was only shrill static.

"For Pete's sake! I wonder who that was?" muttered Chet.

Mr Hardy again adjusted the controls. The static cleared, and the familiar voice came on: "Radley signing off—"

"Wait!" Mr Hardy commanded. "Couldn't catch the last part of your message. Repeat."

"Can you hear me now?"

"Yes."

Radley went on, "Yesterday a float plane was stolen in front of a lodge near Yellowknife. Single engine, colour brown. I will advise progress. Over and out."

"Another theft and a threat," Mr Hardy said in a grim tone, as he leaned forward and snapped off the powerful short-wave set.

"What will you do?" Frank asked his father.

As he waited for an answer, the group was startled by a sudden loud *crash* outside.

"Something's hit the garage!" Joe cried out.

He and Frank dashed from the study and down the stairs. Mr Hardy and the other boys followed the brothers through the kitchen and on to the rear lawn.

"It's our short-wave radio antenna!" Frank shouted, pointing to a high pole near the garage. From it dangled part of the Hardys' three-element-beam antenna over which the detective sent long-distance messages. The rest lay in a jumbled mass of wreckage on the ground.

"What made it fall?" Biff asked in amazement.

"Look!" Joe cried, bending down. "This was no accident!" He held up a twisted strand of rope, one end of which was tied around a metal support.

"Why would anyone want to pull an aerial off the pole?" Tony said, frowning.

"That's what I want to know," declared Mr Hardy. "Get torches and start a search for the vandals. I'll call Chief Collig!"

Joe went into the house with his father, found three torches in a hall cupboard, and rushed outside. The boys beamed their lights on the pole, and Joe held a magnifying glass, trying to detect fingerprints, but found none.

"The vandal must have climbed the pole's spikes to rig the rope," Frank commented.

"And he wore gloves," Joe guessed.

The other boys fanned out over the grounds, hunting for signs of the trespasser, but found nothing. There were not even footprints because the ground was hard and dry.

Just as they turned back towards the house, a police car roared up the driveway, its red roof light flashing. The car stopped and Police Chief Ezra Collig stepped out. The Hardys rushed over to meet him.

"Have you found out who did this, Fenton?" the officer asked.

"Not a clue."

"I'm not surprised," said the tall, husky chief, who had worked closely with Mr Hardy and the boys on several cases. "There has been some vandalism around Bayport lately. This probably is another example of it. Some prankster's idea of fun!"

Frank and Joe glanced at each other.

"I'm afraid it has something to do with Dad's new case," the older boy said.

"Well, maybe," the chief replied. "You would know better about that than I. Just the same, I'll be on the lookout for vandals."

Excitedly speculating on the incident, the brothers and their pals were circling the house again, searching for clues, when they encountered a tall, angular woman coming briskly up the walk.

"Hello, Aunt Gertrude," Frank and Joe greeted their father's sister, who made her home with them. "Have a good time?"

"Yes," she replied. "Our Ladies Guild had an excellent jumble sale."

She dug into her large handbag and brought out two belts with huge silver buckles. "I got these for you boys," Aunt Gertrude told her nephews.

"Wow!" said Joe. "Some present!"

"Thanks, Auntie!" the brothers said together, and Frank added, "Look at those silver buckles! They must be worth a fortune!" He grinned appreciatively. Both Frank and Joe loved their aunt, despite the fact that at times her manner was somewhat peppery and her comments tart.

As Chet, Biff, and Tony crowded round to admire the belts, Aunt Gertrude noticed Chief Collig coming across the lawn with Fenton Hardy. The smile on her face changed to a worried frown.

"Another mystery?" she asked.

The boys explained about the antenna. To allay their aunt's fear, they emphasized the fact that Chief Collig thought it probably was just a prank.

Aunt Gertrude was not to be easily reassured.

"Prank, humph! It's a bad omen, more likely! I hope you'll be careful!"

"We'll watch our step!" said Frank, patting her shoulder.

All the boys returned to Mr Hardy's upstairs study and continued talking of the evening's events. When the detective joined them a few minutes later, he looked serious.

"Time for me to give you the full story," he said. "It will concern each of you."

The boys' excitement mounted at Mr Hardy's words.

"Sam Radley was broadcasting from Yellowknife, in the Canadian Northwest Territories," Fenton Hardy explained, "but we can't communicate now until we get that aerial installed. Radley's investigating a series of thefts which have been taking place at hunting and fishing lodges in the Great Slave Lake area. Rifles, canoes, outboard motors—and now even an aeroplane—have been stolen. The owner of the lodges has retained me to find the thieves. Since I was tied up on something else, he agreed to let my assistant work on it." The detective paused, then continued, "Radley has been up there for some time and—now I think he needs help!"

"I'll go!" each boy volunteered.

Mr Hardy smiled at the response. "I'll need only two of you for the job. Biff and Tony, you can be on your way tomorrow. All expenses paid. If you solve the mystery," he added, "there'll be a bonus!"

Frank, Joe, and Chet looked puzzled. Why weren't they going along? Mr Hardy smiled, and continued, "Don't worry, you three, you're going to Canada too! I need *your* help on another important case!"

"What's that, Dad?" Frank asked eagerly, his face brightening.

"A few days ago," Mr Hardy explained, "I had a telegram from a Mr Black, who is curator of London Museum in England. Because I'd been successful in solving a case in Canada a few years ago, I had been recommended to Mr Black."

"Yes?" Joe prompted.

"This mystery," his father went on, "concerns an invaluable Viking rune stone that was stolen recently in Edmonton, Alberta."

"Wow!" exclaimed Joe. "That's near the edge of the Northwest Territories."

"Those old Scandinavian mariners really covered a lot of water in their far-flung travels," said his father, "often ranging inland for great distances. The runic alphabet was copied from Latin and Greek letters by the Teutonic peoples about the third century. They left permanent messages on stones, and for many centuries afterwards, this stolen one had special significance."

Mr Hardy went on, "It seems a French-Canadian

trapper named Pierre Caron found a stone bearing Viking symbols near the shore of Great Slave Lake. After revealing his find to the press, he contacted the London Museum and the officials there sent an expert on runic symbols, Peter Baker-Jones, to Edmonton to buy the stone for the museum collection. The thieves probably read all about it in the newspapers. A few minutes after Mr Baker-Jones had paid Caron, both men were attacked and robbed. Baker-Jones lost the rune stone, and Caron, his money."

"What about the Edmonton police?" Chet asked. "Are they working on the case?"

"Yes. But despite their efforts and all the help they have had from Caron, they haven't been able to come up with a clue. Baker-Jones is still in a coma."

"Did the telegram say anything else?" Frank asked.

"That's all, Frank. I put through a transatlantic call to Mr Black in London and suggested that the stone probably was already in a museum in Cairo—or some other faraway world capital. But the curator didn't think so because, just before Baker-Jones lost consciousness, he told a doctor that the rune stone symbols contained directions to a Viking treasure hidden in the area."

"And Mr Black thought the thieves would stay around there to look for it?" Frank asked.

"Right!" his father said, smiling.

"Great!" exclaimed Joe, leaping to his feet. "Then we're on the Viking rune stone case?"

"Right again," replied the detective.

The five boys began talking excitedly about the two mysteries. Finally Biff said, "Tony and I had better take off—we have a lot to do to get ready."

"Good idea," Mr Hardy agreed.

Frank, Joe, and Chet hurried downstairs with the two boys.

"Let's cut through the backyard and over the hedge," Tony suggested to Biff as they went outside.

"Sure thing. It's the fastest way home."

The Hardys and Chet waved goodbye to their friends, who hurried off across the yard. The three boys had just turned to go into the house when suddenly they heard a shout.

"Help! Help!"

"It's Biff!" Frank cried out. "Come on, fellows!"

·2·

A Mysterious Label

FRANK, Joe and Chet leaped down the back door steps and dashed to the rear hedge. Both Hardys vaulted it in one fluid motion, while their stout friend pushed his way through.

"Wow!" said Frank. Biff and Tony were kneeling over the motionless form of a man.

Joe pulled a small torch from his pocket and beamed it on the victim. He was a brown-haired man of medium height. "Never saw him before," he said, studying the man's pale face with its pinched features. "And say! He's wearing gloves!"

"Guess he's the pole climber, all right," Frank said.

Noting that the unconscious stranger had a deep gash in his head, Frank whipped out his handkerchief and placed it on the bleeding wound.

"Do you suppose the antenna fell on his head?" Joe asked. "He might be the guy who pulled it down. Started escaping but couldn't make it."

"Anyway, he's hurt," Frank declared. "Let's get him to the hospital right away."

Joe and Chet went to phone for an ambulance, then call Chief Collig and give him a report.

A few minutes later Mr Hardy hurried outside with

the two boys to look at the victim. He said that the injured man was unknown to him also.

Chet told Frank that an ambulance was on its way. "Chief Collig will meet you at Bayport Hospital," he said.

Mr Hardy said he had to go out on a case, so he could not accompany the boys.

When the ambulance arrived, a doctor hopped out and ran to the scene. He quickly examined the unconscious man, then the patient was placed on a stretcher and carried to the ambulance. Frank and Joe received permission to ride with the stranger. Tony, Biff, and Chet said goodbye.

With siren wailing, the ambulance roared through the town of Bayport. In the back, Frank, Joe, and the serious young doctor sat with the patient. A search of the man's pockets produced nothing that would identify him. No wallet, no business card!

As the driver turned the ambulance into the hospital driveway leading to the emergency ramp, the injured man stirred. Frank leaned over. "Can you tell us your name?" he asked.

"J-J-John Kelly," the pale, thin stranger said in a weak voice.

"How were you hurt, Mr Kelly?" Frank queried, as the ambulance came to a halt.

The man grimaced and shook his head. There was no time for further questioning. Two hospital porters pulled open the back doors and lifted out the stretcher. They carried it into the emergency treatment room, where nurses were waiting for the patient.

Frank and Joe hurried to the reception hall, where

they found Chief Collig pacing the floor impatiently. He and a police officer rushed up to the Hardys.

"So you found a man you think might have been the trespasser," the chief said. "Who is he?"

Frank reported the man's name, and the fact that he would say no more. The officer scowled.

"Let's go."

He started down the corridor towards the admissions desk. Here he showed his identification and introduced the Hardys. After a twenty-minute wait a pleasant, efficient sister led the callers to a ground-floor, four-bed room, where the injured stranger, the only occupant, lay in bed.

"The doctor says it will be all right for you to see him," the sister reported and left the room.

Chief Collig looked thoughtful. "John Kelly could very well be an alias," he told the boys. "Since there is no other means of identification, we must take his fingerprints. Want to help me?"

Frank and Joe were efficient at this task and the chief knew it. Frank pressed the sleeping man's thumb and first finger against the edge of a clean water glass. Then the young officer hurried off with the tumbler to check the fingerprint files at headquarters.

Chief Collig and the Hardys returned to the admissions desk to examine Kelly's clothing. The laundry marks and labels in the nondescript tweed jacket and well-worn grey slacks indicated they had been purchased in Bayport.

"Nothing unusual about his clothes," said Frank, disappointed. "It doesn't tell us anything more about him . . . except that he appears to be poor."

"The outfit certainly didn't fit him very well," Joe added. "He probably hasn't eaten much lately."

The chief and the boys thanked the sister for her help, then left the hospital and walked to the waiting police car outside.

"Maybe the fingerprints will be on record," Joe said hopefully, as they drove to headquarters.

But when they arrived, the lieutenant greeted Chief Collig with the news that there were no fingerprints matching Kelly's in the police file. A quick teletype check with the FBI had also been fruitless.

"A blank wall, all right," Joe observed in disgust. "But he sure looks guilty."

"We'll keep on the alert for other clues," Frank declared.

Chief Collig promised that he in turn would circulate a description of Kelly and let the boys know if he learned anything. They said goodbye and were driven home by a policeman.

The brothers found their petite, pretty mother and their Aunt Gertrude waiting for them in the living room. The women looked worried.

"I hate to see you two get mixed up in another dangerous mystery—and your father is still out on his case." Mrs Hardy sighed.

"Yes," sniffed Aunt Gertrude. "I just *know* you'll be hurt one of these days."

Frank and Joe gave both women a hug, and Joe said, "We're still alive and able to eat." He grinned and added, "You know we can take care of ourselves."

It was true. The boys had been involved in many risky adventures since their first case—*The Mystery of the Aztec Warrior.* Recently they had challenged a ruthless band of kidnappers in *The Missing Chums.*

Despite the women's concern for the boys' safety, they obviously were interested as the brothers told of their visit to the hospital. They, too, thought it was significant that there was nothing on the injured man giving an address. When Frank mentioned that the man's worn clothing did not fit him, Aunt Gertrude looked thoughtful.

"There was a man at our guild sale today who bought some used clothing!" she exclaimed. "He didn't seem like the type we usually have as a customer."

Joe broke in eagerly, "Can you describe him, Aunt Gertrude?"

"I remember him clearly. He was very pale and thin. Acted sort of furtive—he'd look away whenever anyone caught his eye. He was well dressed in a black-and-white checked sports jacket and grey slacks, but the clothes he bought were almost threadbare. I was sure they'd be too big."

Frank burst out, "That could have been Kelly. He's pale and thin. His clothes were worn and certainly didn't fit him!"

"Sure!" Joe put in excitedly. "A jumble sale would be the perfect place to buy used clothing if someone wanted to make sure it wouldn't be traced."

"If we could find his ordinary clothes," said Frank, "maybe we'd learn where Kelly comes from."

"You can look for that evidence in the morning," their mother announced quietly. "It *is* late."

Admitting that it had been a long day, the brothers

said good night and went to bed. They fell sound asleep almost instantly.

At breakfast the next morning Frank and Joe told their father of the hospital trip and their suspicions of Kelly. The detective frowned. "I'd certainly like to find out," he said, "what the fellow is up to."

Just then a cheerful whistle sounded from the front lawn, and a moment later Biff Hooper and Tony Prito appeared in the hall.

"We're all set," cried Biff. He waved two plane tickets for that afternoon's flight to Alberta.

"At Edmonton, the capital of the province," Biff explained, "we'll change for Hay River. There we'll pick up a plane going across Great Slave Lake to Yellowknife."

"That's where Sam Radley will meet us. Right, Mr Hardy?" Tony asked.

"Yes. I'll telegram Sam your schedule," the detective replied. "He'll give you the necessary orders when you arrive."

"Great!" Tony grinned, and Biff added, "We'll do our best to carry 'em out."

Both boys thanked Mr Hardy for the chance to work on a case and said goodbye.

"Maybe we'll all get together on these two mysteries," Joe said to his brother as Biff's car pulled away.

"Could be," Frank replied, "but in the meantime let's look for Kelly's discarded clothing. He may have put them in a rubbish bin."

"Right. First place to hunt is the Bayport dump," Joe suggested. "All the town refuse was collected yesterday."

The brothers ran out to the garage and climbed into their newly polished yellow convertible. Frank drove along River Road to the edge of Bayport, where the city dump was located.

As they neared the surrounding fence, the boys could see smoke from the smouldering refuse piles. The Hardys stopped at the main gate, and Joe asked the seated attendant, who was reading a newspaper, where the trash collected the previous day had been dumped.

Pointing to a section of the huge yard, the man said, "Over there!" then returned to his reading.

The boys left their car near the entrance and picked their way across the accumulation of cans, paper, and ashes to the corner area.

"Whew!" Joe looked at the huge pile of trash. "What a job!"

The two young detectives separated and started their search at opposite edges of the mountain of refuse. They worked their way towards the centre of the heap. When they met there, neither boy had found a clue.

Joe looked glum. "Guess we're just out of luck," he said, kicking an old box.

His brother was about to agree, when the box turned over and out fell a rolled-up pair of grey slacks. Both boys grabbed for the box and Frank pulled out a black-and-white checked sports jacket.

"Wa-hoo!" Frank exulted, holding up the jacket and turning it inside out. "Look at this label—Toronto, Canada!"

"The slacks are from Quebec," Joe said, looking puzzled. "Do you think Kelly is from Canada?"

"He could be," Frank answered, greatly excited.

"Between the ruined aerial and this evidence I'd certainly say Kelly has something to do with Dad's case up there!"

The discussion was suddenly interrupted by a piercing *zoing-g-g* as a rifle bullet whined past them into the dump pile!

"Down!" cried Frank. Both boys dived to their stomachs behind a dusty mound of ashes. They lay still, their hearts pounding. Who could be shooting at them?

After a few minutes Frank cautiously raised his head. Coming across the edge of the dump towards them was a man carrying a rifle. A fat brown beagle trotted behind him.

The Hardys leaped to their feet, and Joe started forward, his face flushed with anger. Frank grabbed his brother's arm. "Just a minute, Joe. I don't think the man was shooting at us deliberately."

The man was now running towards the brothers. "D-did I hit anybody?" he wavered. "I was shooting rats and—and I didn't see you two—honest!"

Frank and Joe relaxed somewhat. "No," Frank said tersely, "you didn't hit us. But you'd better be more careful after this when you're aiming a gun."

The relieved rifleman stuttered an apology as the Hardys picked up the slacks and jacket and hurried off to their car.

"Let's go to the hospital right after lunch," Joe urged as they drove away, "and see Kelly's reaction to this clothing!"

After a quick lunch, the boys asked Aunt Gertrude to go with them to identify Kelly, and headed for the hospital. When they arrived, it was too early for the usual visiting hours, but the sister, knowing of the Hardys, led the way to Kelly's ground-floor room. The door was closed.

As they neared it, Frank said, "Hold the clothes behind you, Joe. I'll try to catch him off guard first with some questions!"

Joe nodded and turned the knob, pushing the door open. The boys and their aunt stared aghast. *The hospital room was empty!* The sister wheeled and hurried down the hall to get help.

Frank pointed wordlessly to the open window and the brothers darted towards it.

"There goes Kelly with someone!" exclaimed Frank.

He pointed to a thin man in a long overcoat, pulled-down hat, and sneakers hurrying across the lawn with a red-haired companion. They were heading towards a waiting green car. Kelly opened the door and both men quickly got in.

"Come on, Joe! We must catch them!" Frank urged as he swung himself out of the window.

·3·

Rune Stone Curse

JOE jumped out of the hospital window and joined Frank who by now was sprinting across the grassy lawn after the escaped patient. They were too late to capture Kelly. The getaway car was already roaring off down the tree-lined street.

"Let's chase them!" Frank cried out.

He ran up the street to the boys' convertible and jumped behind the wheel. Joe hopped in beside him. Frank turned on the ignition, swung the yellow car out from the kerb, and raced after the speeding saloon. It turned a corner.

For a while the brothers were afraid the car had eluded them, but suddenly they spotted it a few blocks ahead. "Let's hope we don't get any red lights," Frank murmured.

The chase continued through Bayport and on to the main road out of town. Frank pressed the accelerator to the floor. Soon they were out in the open country. The green car was still in sight.

"We're in luck!" Joe exclaimed, pointing to the left.

A long freight train was rumbling down the railway tracks which crossed the road just ahead. The crossing gates were starting to lower.

"Now we'll catch Kelly and find out what's going on," Frank gloated.

The green saloon was almost at the crossing. Putting on an extra burst of speed, the car raced across the tracks. It avoided the gates by inches. Seconds later, the train roared by.

"We've missed our chance," Frank groaned as he braked to a stop.

"There are at least eighty cars!" Joe grumbled over the noise of the wheels and the shrill sound of the train's whistle.

The brothers shifted impatiently in the front seat of their car while they watched the train go by— *clickety-clack, clickety-clack.* Finally it passed them and the gates were raised.

Frank started the car again, and drove across the tracks. As they expected, the green car was nowhere in sight.

"Those guys have a big lead on us now," Joe said. "But let's follow, anyway."

About five miles farther on, Frank brought his car to a halt. "It's no use, Joe," he said quietly, and turned the convertible back towards Bayport. "They could have turned off on to any of these side roads."

"I wonder who Kelly's pal is?" asked Joe. "Kelly must have got word to him somehow."

"The redheaded man could have come to the hospital and roamed around until he found Kelly," Frank suggested.

"Kelly's leaving that way sure makes him suspect," Joe remarked.

The boys had almost reached the railroad tracks

when Joe, glancing from his window, exclaimed, "Stop! There's the green saloon!" He pointed to a tree-shaded culvert running at right angles to the road.

Instantly Frank stopped the car. The boys leaped from the convertible and ran across the macadam road for a better look. The car was well hidden by the bushes and trees.

A quick glance told the Hardys that the car was empty. "Kelly and his friend must have jumped on to the train," Frank commented, as he wrote down the car's licence number. "If only we could stop the train!"

"Why not?" asked Joe. "Chief Collig can arrange that!"

The boys ran back to their car and drove on quickly until they reached a petrol station, where Frank called the police chief.

"Here's news for you, Frank," said Chief Collig. "That saloon was stolen this morning." The chief said he would call ahead to the stationmaster at the next stop—ten miles ahead—to have the freight train delayed until the Hardys could search it. "Good luck!" the official said.

With Joe taking a turn at the wheel, the yellow convertible sped along a narrow dirt road which was a shortcut to the next station.

"It's here!" Frank cried out.

The freight train was slowing to a halt at the small platform. It took the Hardys only a moment to explain to the stationmaster and the train conductor what they wanted.

"It's no use looking in the locked cars, they couldn't

get in there," the conductor said, "but there are some empties."

Led by the two men, the brothers hurried down the tracks, searching the open, empty cars. There were half a dozen of them, but none contained the suspects. The brothers were very disappointed.

"Guess you're out of luck, fellows," said the conductor, who was about to signal to the driver to move the train on.

"Wait!" Joe called, as he ran round the guards' van check the other side of the freight train. A door of one of the supposedly closed cars was open.

Frank followed and both boys climbed inside. At one end of the sawdust-covered floor was a huge pile of empty grain sacks. The brothers ran forward eagerly, hoping to find their quarry hidden behind them. But neither Kelly nor his accomplice was there. Disappointed, Frank went to the carriage door and hopped down. Joe walked over, slowly shaking his head in perplexity.

Suddenly Frank whirled round and called, "Jump, Joe! Jump!"

At the same instant the train gave a forward lurch ahead. Joe hurled himself towards the opening and leaped out just as the heavy sliding door slammed shut behind him.

"Wow!" Frank watched the train slowly gather speed. "Guess the conductor didn't hear you. The weight of that door could kill someone!"

"And I was nearly the one!" Joe said wryly and he gave a whistle of relief at his narrow escape.

The boys walked back to their car and started for

Bayport. Each was thinking, "Was Kelly ever on the train? If so, when did he get off? Or did he flee in some other direction after abandoning the stolen saloon?"

When the boys reached home, Frank called police headquarters and reported their failure to find Kelly to Chief Collig.

Next, they gave their father a full account of the fugitive's disappearance, and the discovery of the clothes from Toronto and Quebec.

Mr Hardy immediately sent a telegram to the Edmonton police with a description of the fugitive and stressed the possibility that the man might be wearing a bandage on his head.

Then the detective turned to the boys and smiled. "Which makes you all the more eager to start for Canada, I'll bet!"

"Right, Dad!" Frank said, grinning.

"May we leave tomorrow morning?" Joe asked excitedly.

"Sorry, son," said Mr Hardy. "You'll need the next few days to get ready."

"*That* long?" Frank looked dismayed.

His father's eyes twinkled. "Yes. You see, boys, your pilot's licences are for land planes—and you're going to require seaplane ratings for this trip. I want you to know how to handle a float plane, if the necessity arises."

"But Dad, we already know how to fly," Frank cried in protest.

Mr Hardy smiled. "And skilfully, too. But take-offs and landings are a bit different with a seaplane, since you're dealing with a variable runway—water—which may be rough."

"You're right, Dad. I didn't think of that. When do we start?" Joe asked.

"Jack Wayne said he could begin your training tomorrow," Mr Hardy replied. "You're to meet him at the field."

Jack was a private pilot whom the detective often used on long trips in the Hardy plane. He had taught Frank and Joe to fly and had been involved in many of their exciting adventures.

"Oh—oh," came the voice of Aunt Gertrude from the doorway. "More trouble. Now you're talking about landing on the water. It sounds very dangerous! Far too dangerous, if you ask me."

"How about a flight while we try it?" Joe teased.

"No, thank you. I prefer cooking. I came to tell you dinner's ready."

After the meal of juicy, tender roast beef, buttered baked potatoes, fresh asparagus, and chocolate cake, the boys excused themselves to study the Canadian map in their atlas. Just as they turned to the proper page, a rattle of metal and a short *beep* from the street made the boys smile. "Chet's jalopy," Joe said with a laugh.

A minute later their chubby friend walked into the living room. "Hi, fellows!"

"You look worried," Frank said. "Is something the matter?"

Chet shook his head. "I'd love to go to Canada with you, but I think I'll change my mind."

"What!" the brothers chorused. "Why?"

Their chunky friend rolled his eyes dramatically. "I've been reading up on rune stones, and boy oh boy, are they unlucky!"

"Unlucky?" Joe echoed.

"Yes, *sir*," said Chett. "And the Horkel stone, which is the most evil of them all"—he paused for emphasis— "was found right near where you're going!"

·4·

Dangerous Solo

"AN evil stone!" Joe broke into a wide grin. "You don't really *believe* all those superstitious legends, do you, Chet?" he asked.

"Well—I'm not sure—but I don't believe in taking chances."

"You can say that again," Joe teased.

"Tell us about this Horkel stone," Frank encouraged Chet. "It sounds interesting."

"Yes, I'd like to hear the story, too," said Mr Hardy, who had just walked into the room.

Chet's worried look disappeared, and, obviously enjoying himself, he began. "Well, I asked Miss Shannon at the library for some information, and she lent me a terrific book about the Vikings and their rune tablets. The word 'rune,' by the way," Chet added importantly, "meant 'secret' in the Anglo-Saxon language."

"How about the Horkel stone?" Joe questioned.

"Oh, that one was named after a Danish Viking called Horkel who settled in Greenland with the expedition of Lief the Lucky." Chet warmed to his story. "The stone had been cursed centuries before by a Saxon priest when one of Horkel's ancestors stole it from him. Its evil history was so well known that Lief made Horkel and his followers go in a different ship, and even settle farther up the fiord than any of the other families.

"Then"—Chet's voice grew louder with enthusiasm —"Lief and his men left Greenland, but they didn't take Horkel's group along. Nobody ever saw the stone again."

"But—" Joe tried to break in.

"Until," Chet continued, "a few years ago an Indian found a tablet bearing strange characters near the base of Alexandra Falls, on Hay River, up in the Northwest Territories. The characters were thought to be runic, and they were translated. There's been a lot of disagreement over whether or not the stone is authentic, but one thing's sure—it has brought terrible misfortune to all the people who owned it."

"Like what?" Joe demanded, half fascinated, half sceptical.

"Like mysterious deaths, and fires, and accidents," Chet answered, his eyes wide with excitement.

"That's a strange story, all right," put in Mr Hardy, leaning forward in his chair. "Even without jinxed stones, that area is dangerous."

"What do you mean, Dad?" Frank asked.

"Just south of Great Slave Lake is the famous Wood Buffalo National Park," said the detective, "where the world's largest buffalo herd lives in refuge, protected by the Canadian government. The wood buffalo is a savage, treacherous animal, ready at all times to charge like a mad bull. It's an enormous beast—black and shaggy. The park is also the home of the arctic fox, the arctic wolf, and sometimes the dangerous northern plains grizzly bear. It's beautiful country, but untamed!"

"Wow!" Joe exclaimed. "There's nothing small up *there!*"

"Oh, yes, there is," Mr Hardy went on, "but sometimes the smallest things are the most dangerous and troublesome."

"What are they?" asked Chet in surprise.

"Insects," Mr Hardy answered. "The bigger animals are usually kept under control, but the gnats, mosquitoes, and black flies are a real problem. Even though they're small, they can be very vicious, especially the black flies. They have been known to kill unprotected men and animals by stinging them to death."

"Sure must be rugged!" Joe remarked, impressed. "We'll have to take mosquito netting along."

Chet eyed him suspiciously. "Don't sound so happy about it! You may not be so cheerful when you get there!"

Mr Hardy leaned over the atlas on the table and pointed out to the boys exactly where Great Slave Lake was in relation to Edmonton.

With a wink at his brother, Joe said to Chet, "We'll send you a snapshot of the unlucky rune stone if we come across it."

For a moment the plump boy's face was a study of conflicting emotions. Then a slow grin spread over his features.

"Okay, fellows, you win!" he declared. "I'm not going to be scared out of the trip by any little old stone. Count me in!"

Mr Hardy and his sons laughed. "That's the spirit, Detective Morton!" The older sleuth cheered him. They were still grinning when Chet left.

The next morning Frank and Joe started for the airport right after an early breakfast, eager to begin their float plane lessons. At the field, Jack Wayne greeted the boys with a warm handshake and smile.

"Ready for lesson number one?" he asked with a grin.

"You bet."

Jack took them over to the seaplane dock, where a sleek, four-seater plane was moored. Here he showed the brothers the construction of the pontoons on the craft. Next, he explained the function of the water rudder, saying it helped steer the plane while taxiing.

"Let's take her up," Jack suggested, "and you'll see the difference between land planes and float planes in action."

The three climbed inside and the pilot taxied the aircraft out over the choppy waters of Barmet Bay.

"Always watch for floating objects on take-off," Jack cautioned the Hardys. "They're usually the cause of accidents."

The craft planed along the water, throwing a spray from either side. When they were in the air, Jack gave the controls first to Frank, then to Joe. Both boys found the landing and take-off procedures quite different from a conventional aeroplane.

"In take-off," explained Jack Wayne, "you must use enough power to get the plane 'on the step,' or planing."

Frank looked puzzled. "That means," went on Wayne, "that you give it enough speed so the plane is riding on just the very bottom section of the float."

"Then it's planing on top of the water?" asked Joe.

"Exactly," agreed the instructor. "When you're on the step, all you need is a little back pressure on the stick and you're airborne."

"Is there ever any trouble?" Joe queried.

"Not really. If the water is a dead flat calm, it's sometimes difficult to get the plane on the step. The surface tension will hold it down."

"Then what?" questioned Frank.

"Just push the stick to one side very gently, keeping your rudder bar in the centre position. This gentle, even pressure will lift one float out of the water."

"Then pull back on the stick and off you go," said Frank.

"Right. Now, Frank, I want you to try a couple of solo take-offs and landings. Joe and I'll be waiting on the dock."

Frank grinned in anticipation as Jack landed. After Jack Wayne and Joe had stepped out, Frank manned the craft alone. He had no trouble taking off, because there was enough chop on the bay for him to get up on the step easily.

Frank loved the exhilaration of piloting a plane. His first landing went well, and he thrilled at the way the pontoons dropped stern first into the water.

As Frank took off the second time, he waved his wings to Jack and Joe. After circling twice, Frank turned for his second landing. Jack's instructions went through his mind—line up plenty of water, back gently on the throttle, lower the water rudder. Finally, centre the stick and rudder and let her stall in.

As the aircraft slapped into the water, Frank eased the throttle ahead a fraction. He was going to keep it up on the step and plane across the bay so Joe could have a turn.

The aircraft bounced easily on the step, and as he skipped across the water, he felt the tremendous sensation of speed. Frank pulled the throttle back to cut the power, and pressed the rudder bar to turn the aircraft into the wind towards the dock. As the plane started to veer, he suddenly remembered Jack's warning:

"Never try turning into the wind if the aircraft is moving at high speed," Jack had said.

It was too late!

Bang! Frank felt the jerk as the starboard wing dipped into the water. As he glanced out, the plane's nose dipped into the bay, and his head crashed against the dashboard. The water came rushing up at him.

"Frank crashed!" yelled Joe, staring in horror at the overturned float plane.

"Quick—into my outboard!" Jack urged. He and Joe ran to a small motorboat tied up nearby.

In less than a minute the boat was speeding out over the bay towards the plane, which lay on its side, one wing pointing in the air.

By the time they reached it, Joe had his shirt and shoes off. As Jack throttled down, Joe dived over the side and swam underwater to the submerged cockpit.

Desperately Joe wrenched the door of the aircraft open. He groped wildly for the seat belt, which he unfastened. Then, bracing his feet against the doorframe, Joe grabbed Frank's shoulders and pulled him free.

Joe's lungs were ready to burst as he dragged his brother to the surface. When they broke through, Jack was leaning over the side of the boat. He reached for Frank and hauled him aboard. Joe scrambled up and applied artificial respiration while Jack raced the boat to shore.

Suddenly Frank stirred and both rescuers gave a sigh of relief.

"Don't try *that* stunt again!" Joe grinned at his brother, but inwardly shuddered as he thought of Frank's close call.

"No fear of that!" Frank grinned back. "One crack on the noggin's enough!"

When they reached shore, Frank insisted he felt well enough to drive home. His only injury was a bruise on his forehead. "Hope I didn't put your plane out of commission, Jack," he said.

"I'm sure the mechanics can fix it up," Jack replied, adding that he would have the craft refloated immediately.

Frank smiled wanly at Joe. "I ruined your chance to do a solo. Sorry."

"I'll get a turn," Joe said cheerfully.

The boys returned home and hurried up to their room without encountering their mother or aunt. They showered and put on dry clothes.

At the dinner table the boys' family commented on Frank's darkening bruise. The brothers told of Frank's miscalculation, but made light of the incident.

Later that evening, while they were studying the

maps of the Great Slave Lake area, the phone rang. Joe answered and a woman at the other end of the line said:

"This is Miss Shannon at the public library. Chet Morton mentioned that you boys are interested in Viking rune stones. I was wondering if you took out one of our reference books on the subject by mistake."

"No, I didn't," said Joe. "What book is it?"

"One of the most valuable in our collection," Miss Shannon replied. "*Rune Stones and Viking Symbols* by Peter Baker-Jones."

Detective's Double

At the name Peter Baker-Jones, Joe was instantly alert. "The man in the Edmonton hospital!" he recalled. "The one who bought the rune stone and was knocked out."

And now a valuable book by Baker-Jones was missing from the Bayport Library!

"Are you still on the line?" Miss Shannon's voice broke into his thoughts.

"Oh—sorry," Joe apologized. "Frank and I don't have the book. But I'd like very much to know who took it."

"So would we," the librarian said sadly. "Well, I thought I'd just ask you about it to make sure."

Joe said goodbye and replaced the telephone in its stand. He walked slowly back to the living room.

"What's up?" Frank asked, seeing the puzzled look on his brother's face. Quickly Joe explained.

"This means," Frank said excitedly, "there's someone else here in Bayport who's interested in the missing rune stone! *If* the book was stolen, that is."

"I have a hunch it was," Joe stated. "Frank, do you think Kelly could have had something to do with this case, as well as the one Radley has been working on?"

"He certainly could. And the book may be just what the thieves need to figure out the runic symbols."

Just then the doorbell rang. It was Chet. The Hardys told him about Miss Shannon's call. Chet listened carefully, then said, "I looked over the complete collection of Viking books, and I don't remember seeing that title. The one by Baker-Jones must have been taken before I was there."

"Which could have been before our aerial was pulled down," Frank said. "By this time the book might be in Canada."

"Maybe you'll know for sure the day after tomorrow," came Mr Hardy's voice from the doorway.

"You mean we'll leave for Edmonton then?" Joe asked excitedly.

"Yes." The detective said that he had overheard the boys' discussion of the missing book. "So I think you three had better get started north and see what you can learn from Mr Baker-Jones," the detective concluded with a smile.

"That'll be our first step," Frank said.

The boys stayed up talking about their trip and speculating on the mysteries until Chet began to yawn.

"I'd better get all the sleep I can now," Chet defended himself. "I probably won't get a wink up in that wilderness." With that, he left for home.

The next morning after breakfast Frank and Joe drove again to the airport. First they made plane reservations for their trip, then met Jack Wayne for more float plane lessons. The pilot took them up for some aerobatics.

They stopped for lunch, then returned to the plane.

Frank and Joe each made six take-offs and landings. By the end of the practice, Jack said they were skilled enough to pass the compulsory proficiency test which was set by the FAA, the Federal Aviation Administration, which governs all matters concerning civil aviation in the US.

"What about floating debris on night landings?" asked Frank.

"There's nothing you can do about that." Wayne laughed. "If you're landing in a strange lake or river, you just have to take a chance there isn't any."

That night each of the boys made six landings. Though they had done it often during the day, they found the experience an eerie one.

"Just decrease your speed until the plane begins to fall, and maintain a three-point attitude," Wayne instructed. "Give yourself lots of room and come down flying. The only secret is to cut your throttle the moment the floats skim into the water."

After a late snack the Hardys packed, then went to bed. They were tired from the full day's flying, and wanted to be awake to leave early the next day.

Frank and Joe got up greatly refreshed. They were just finishing breakfast when Chet arrived. The three boys were given last-minute advice and fond hugs by Aunt Gertrude, then were driven to the seaplane dock by Mr and Mrs Hardy.

There the brothers took the FAA test, which they passed with flying colours, and had SES, for single-engine seaplane, inscribed on their licences.

Then Mr and Mrs Hardy drove the boys to the airport. After checking the luggage, Frank, Joe, and

Chet shook hands with the detective. "Good luck on your part of the mystery, boys," he said. "Be on your guard every minute. I'll be checking with you."

"Right, Dad," Joe said, and Frank added, "We'll get on the case as soon as we land."

Chet grinned. "That's for sure!"

Mrs Hardy, although always a bit worried when her sons set off on a new mission, smiled as she kissed them all goodbye. "Do take care of yourselves," she cautioned.

A few minutes later the boys boarded the silver jet plane for Edmonton. By midday the plane was over Winnipeg and the passengers could see the wide prairies below. The flight had been smooth so far.

Joe was seated next to the window, enjoying the magnificent view. Frank and Chet were reading the flight-guide pamphlets. The stillness was broken by an announcement over the loudspeaker:

"Ladies and gentlemen, this is your captain speaking. Because of bad weather and turbulence over Edmonton, we are landing at Saskatoon. The delay probably will be overnight, but the stewardesses will give you complete details of your departure time and accommodations. Please fasten your seat belts."

Within minutes the stewardesses had checked the passengers' belts and the jetliner began its descent. Frank pointed out the illustrations in the pamphlet of Saskatoon and the Canadian Air Force training craft stationed there.

As they dropped over the runway, Joe leaned close to the window for a better view. "There's one of the training planes now!" He pointed to a dark-grey craft landing on a parallel runway.

At that moment there was a *swo-o-o-sh* as the jetliner levelled out and the wheels caught the field. Joe craned his neck to watch the grey plane.

Suddenly there was a loud *swish* and a *bang*, and the tyre of the jet's starboard side blew out. The plane rocked violently to one side.

Wh-a-am! Joe was thrown against the window, hitting his head on the frame. He saw swirling lights, then everything went black.

When Joe opened his eyes and things began to come back into focus, he looked up into the face of a stewardess who was dabbing his forehead with a cold, wet cloth.

"What happened?" he asked dazedly.

"You hit your head!" the girl said, looking concerned. "Are you all right?"

"I think I am now," Joe said, grinning. "No permanent dents!"

"Don't scare us like that again, boy," said Frank, as he and Chet smiled in relief.

"That'll teach me to look out the window when we're landing." Joe ruefully rubbed his throbbing head.

When they disembarked, the three boys were directed to a modern Saskatoon hotel. En route, they made a tour of the city and saw its mammoth grain elevators.

Chet grinned. "They look like out-of-place skyscrapers!"

The following morning dawned clear and sunny. The jet left promptly, and after an uneventful trip, arrived in Edmonton by midday. The large airport there was busy with flights to and from Alaska, northern Canada, and the United States.

Before the Hardys and Chet disembarked they learned from a stewardess that Edmonton is the focal point of the mining and fur-producing regions of the Arctic. "Also," she added, "it's a busy agricultural distributing centre."

The pleasant young woman wished them an enjoyable stay, then the three boys headed for the airport terminal building.

After claiming their luggage, they found a hotel and booked in. Then Frank said, "Now to visit Mr Baker-Jones."

They took a taxi to the Edmonton hospital. Here they were referred to the sister on the first floor. When they inquired about Peter Baker-Jones, she said:

"I'm sorry, but you can't see him. Mr Baker-Jones is still in a coma, and as I told his other caller, we don't know how long it will be until he regains consciousness, poor man."

" 'Other caller'!" Frank echoed. "Who was it?"

"A man named Fenton Hardy," replied the nurse. "He left just a few minutes ago."

"Dad?" Frank and Joe stared at each other.

"It couldn't have been," Chet said, "unless your father took the next flight and wasn't stopped by the bad weather."

"He never mentioned coming this soon," Frank declared. "There's a phone booth. I'm going to call home and find out about this."

Joe and Chet thought it a good idea and Frank

placed the call to Bayport. Mr Hardy answered the phone!

Frank burst out, "I knew you weren't here, Dad!"

"What do you mean by that?" Mr Hardy asked with a slight chuckle. "Did you think I was?"

"No," Frank replied, and explained, "One of the sisters here at the Edmonton hospital told us you had been, and I'm sure many other people heard Fenton Hardy was here too. Dad, some man is impersonating you. He was just here trying to see Baker-Jones."

"Be very careful," cautioned Mr Hardy, instantly serious. "I don't know why anyone would pose as me, unless it was to get some further valuable information from the Englishman in connection with the rune stone."

"At least we're tipped off," Frank answered. He assured his father that the boys were well and explained why the flight had arrived a day late.

"Check with the police and try to locate the man who found the rune stone," the detective suggested, when he learned that the Englishman had not regained consciousness.

Frank said goodbye and returned to Chet and Joe. When Joe heard that his father was home, he immediately hurried to the nurse and asked her for a description of Mr Baker-Jones's caller. Her meagre description could fit Fenton Hardy or hundreds of other men.

"No clue there," he reported to the boys.

Discussing their next move, the trio started towards the lift.

"I suppose the best place to get details of the attack on Baker-Jones is at police headquarters," Frank said. "Let's check there."

The boys were talking excitedly as they rounded the corner of the brightly lighted hall. They collided head on with a huge brawny figure.

"*Bon tonnerre!*" he exclaimed in a deep booming voice. "What's this?"

The speaker was a powerful-looking man, well over six feet tall. His strong-featured face was covered by a thick, black beard, and he wore a red-and-black checkered wool shirt, dark trousers and heavy, laced boots.

Joe staggered backwards from the impact, bumping against the wall. The stranger reached out a huge hand, grasped Joe by the arm, and steadied him on his feet.

"*Bon tonnerre!*" he shouted again.

· 6 ·

Canadian Giant

THE huge fingers holding Joe's arm were like a steel vice.

"So-o sorry," he apologized, staring up at the bearded man with whom he had collided. To his relief, Joe felt the powerful fingers relax their grip.

"Carefully, here!" boomed the stranger in a strong French-Canadian accent. "You should always look where you're going—especially in a hospital!"

"We realize that, sir," Frank spoke up. "But we were hurrying to get to the police station."

"Ah, the police," the big man said. His eyes narrowed. "You were here to see Monsieur Baker-Jones, yes?"

The three boys said yes. Joe recovered his breath as the big man studied the visitors for a moment. His eyes were piercing, black, and shaded by thick brows.

"You're Pierre Caron!" Frank exclaimed suddenly.

The man stepped back warily, as he answered, "*Oui*, I am Pierre Caron, but I am called 'Caribou.' " He cocked his head and asked curiously, "Who are *you*?"

Frank introduced himself, Joe, and Chet, then explained the reason why they had come to see Baker-Jones.

"Does he speak now?" Caribou asked abruptly.

"No," Joe answered him. "The sister said he's still in a coma."

"*Bon tonnerre!*" the fur trapper exploded. "That is not good." He added that he had been given special permission by Baker-Jones's doctor to visit the patient briefly every day. "But he never change," the woodsman added sadly. "I hoped today he would be better."

Frank told Caribou that they would like to hear his account of the assault by the rune stone thieves.

"We will talk while we eat," Caribou said. He smiled broadly. "Come! Let us go!"

The powerful giant marched ahead to the lift, which took them to the reception hall. He pushed open the heavy front door and went on without breaking stride.

The three boys had to trot to keep up with Caribou, and they were still a few yards behind when he stopped at a crowded restaurant. As the trapper strode towards a table, three burly men shouted greetings to him from across the room. He grinned and waved to them vigorously.

"My friends from the north," he said to the boys.

The big French-Canadian ordered a meal of steak, potatoes, and gravy for all. "First we eat," he said, when Joe started to ask questions.

The Hardys and Chet grinned at one another. Instinctively they liked this excitable, forthright man of the woods.

After they had finished the hearty meal, Caribou leaned back in his chair and relaxed. Frank quickly explained his father's connection with the rune stone case and asked Pierre Caron for details of the robbery.

"Monsieur Baker-Jones asked me to come to his hotel

room," Caribou began. "I went and gave him the stone. He handed me two thousand dollars—in new one-hundred-dollar bills. I signed a paper saying he had paid me. Then *bon tonnerre!* two men rushed into the room." The trapper stopped to drink some hot coffee.

"What did they look like?" Chet asked.

Caribou wiped his beard with a red handkerchief and pushed his chair back from the table again. In his excitement he began to speak in his native patois.

"I could not see faces. Both wear rubber face masks. One man was very thin. He was wearing checked jacket—black and white. Other man wear dark city clothes."

The boys were excited. "Then what?" Joe urged him.

"Thin man's pal never speak. He waved gun," Caribou continued, "and force me to corner of room. *Bon tonnerre!*" His voice grew angry. "The thin man want the stone. When Monsieur Baker-Jones say no, he hit him on the head with a gun!"

The woodsman told the boys that the Englishman had collapsed. As Caribou had bent over him to help, the two gunmen had fled with the rune stone and the two thousand dollars.

The Hardys exchanged quick glances. Frank voiced their thought aloud. "The thin fellow could be a man we know as John Kelly!" The brothers told Caribou the story.

"He is a slippery eel!" growled the trapper. "You think he come back here?"

"I wouldn't doubt it," Frank replied. "We aim to find him, anyway!"

"Where did you find the rune stone?" Joe asked Caribou.

The boys listened intently to his story. "I run my trapline between Fort Smith and Great Slave Lake," he began. "Two, three weeks ago I made trip to the north end of the lake. I find the stone on the beach and—"

Suddenly the burly giant broke off. He sprang up from his chair violently, knocking over the table. Dishes and glasses flew in all directions, shattering on the floor as Caribou dashed to the front door.

"Come on!" Frank urged, leaping up.

The three boys dashed outside. When they reached Caribou he was standing on the pavement in front of the restaurant, his fists clenched and his cheeks flushed with anger.

"*Bon tonnerre!*" he boomed in rage. "*Sacre bleu!*"

"What happened?" Joe asked. "Did you spot one of the thieves?"

"No. But I saw Dulac," Caribou said, still looking up and down the street. "The weasel! He robs my traps. If I catch him—*bon tonnerre!*—that will be his unlucky day!"

As they all walked back into the restaurant to pay their bill and settle for the broken dishes, Caribou explained that Abner Dulac also was a trapper. He had been stealing from Caribou's traps up north for a long time. Caribou once had given him a thrashing, but the big woodsman had never been able to catch him with any evidence.

"What's Dulac doing in Edmonton?" Frank asked.

"I don't know," Caribou replied. "Probably he sell my pelts—or maybe he here to get even with me for that beating!" The giant shook his head disgustedly, then shrugged. "I forget him for now," he said, and asked the boys, "Where you think to look for the men who robbed Monsieur Baker-Jones and me?"

The Hardys said they thought perhaps the thieves would have travelled north to hide out with their loot.

Caribou pounded his fist into the palm of his hand. "Then I will be your guide," he offered. "I will help trap the robbers!"

"That would be great," Joe said with a grin. "We'll need a guide in that country."

"I'll say!" Chet declared thankfully.

"Our next move is to find out what the police here can tell us about the missing rune stone," Frank said. "Come on!"

Caribou led the way, stalking along the sidewalks as though he were still in the wilderness. At the ultra-modern police headquarters the Hardys were directed to the office of Inspector Knight. He had no new information for them, however. The Edmonton police, working with the Mounties, had traced all the leads they had on the missing rune stone and stolen cash, but so far without success.

"The last we heard," said the inspector, "was that a man with a gauze patch on his head had been seen in McMurray up the Athabasca River. But he disappeared before we could question him."

"Kelly again, I'll bet!" Joe exclaimed.

Quickly the Hardys revealed to the inspector their encounter with the suspect in Bayport, and their hunch he might have returned to the Northwest Territories.

"He may still be wearing a bandage on his head," Frank said.

The official was keenly interested. "I'll have the fellow's description broadcast again."

Frank also reported that a man purporting to be Fenton Hardy had wanted to see Mr Baker-Jones in the hospital. The officer made a note of this and wished the sleuths good luck.

Caribou accompanied the boys to their hotel. When they walked into the foyer, the receptionist stopped them.

"Are you Frank and Joe Hardy?" he asked the brothers.

"Yes."

The man reached behind him into one of the guest mailboxes.

"Here's a telephone message for you," he said, handing Frank an envelope.

"What could it be?" Chet asked, peering over Frank's shoulder as he took out the note.

"It's from home!" Frank exclaimed, as he read the note aloud: " '*Phone immediately. Plans changed.*' "

·7·

White Water

THE Hardys stared at the message in concern. "I hope there's nothing wrong at home," Joe said, looking worried.

The boys and Caribou hurried upstairs to the hotel room, and Frank called Bayport. Mr Hardy answered the phone. After reassuring his son that everyone was fine, he explained, "I had a coded message from Sam Radley after your phone call. He received a report yesterday that an unidentified man bought ten drums of aviation fuel and two drums of oil at the Hudson's Bay Company store in Fort Smith."

"That's on the Slave River," Frank said. "It runs north into Great Slave Lake."

"Right," his father replied. "The man had the fuel delivered to a raft on the river, and Sam thinks he might be the one who stole the small float plane at Yellowknife." The detective paused. "Biff, Tony and Sam are busy on another lead, so I'd like you boys to track down this one. If you get up there fast," he continued, "you might be able to pick up the trail and find the hideout of the thieves around Great Slave Lake."

"We'll leave pronto, Dad," Frank said eagerly. "We planned to go there, anyway—on our own case.

Caribou Caron is with us, and he has offered to be our guide."

"That's fine," said Mr Hardy. "Have you seen the Edmonton police?"

"Yes," Frank replied, "but they've had no success on the rune stone mystery. They had a report of a thin man with a gauze patch on his head at McMurray, but lost him there. Sounds as if he's the man who got away from us in Bayport."

"That settles it. The sooner you and Caron get started for Fort Smith, the better!" the detective said. "Good luck!"

When Frank relayed Mr Hardy's news to the others, Caribou slapped Joe so hard on the back the boy winced. *"Bon tonnerre!"* the giant cried. "This is the right kind of adventure for trapper. I have been in the city too long."

Frank suggested that before leaving, he and Joe return to the hospital and show the staff a picture of their father and warn them about the man posing as Fenton Hardy.

"In the meantime, Chet," Frank continued, "you get plane reservations to Fort Smith on the first flight out. We'll meet you back at the hotel."

Caribou said that he would do an errand. "I must buy new boots for the trip."

When the Hardys arrived at the hospital, they quickly found the sister in charge of the first floor and Frank showed her the snapshot of his father. "This is the real Fenton Hardy," he said politely. "The man who wanted to visit Mr Baker-Jones was an impostor."

"Impostor!" the nurse exclaimed in alarm. "Why, I never suspected—oh dear!"

"Luckily no harm was done," Frank assured her. "But please tell everyone that Fenton Hardy will *not* call on Mr Baker-Jones."

The sister promised to warn the rest of the staff. Their next stop was at Edmonton police headquarters, where they found Inspector Knight at his desk.

"We've just talked to our father," Frank explained. "Our plans have changed. We're flying to Fort Smith. We'll contact you if anything breaks there. And would you let us know if the impostor shows up again?"

Inspector Knight assured the boys that if the man was spotted, he would get in touch with them through the Hudson's Bay Company at Fort Smith.

The Hardys thanked him and hurried back to the hotel.

"Reservations all set," Chet reported. "Nothing for today. Take-off's at ten tomorrow. I've told Caribou, and he'll meet us here."

The next morning the four set off for the airport. Their plane left on schedule. Minutes after they were airborne, Joe nudged Chet and pointed to the ground.

"Look!" he said excitedly. "We're already over wilderness."

The landscape below was barren and the prairie looked desolate. What few trees there were appeared as dark patches on the brown earth.

After short stopovers at McMurray and Uranium City, the plane touched down at Fort Smith. This was familiar territory to Caribou and he took charge immediately.

"Only two taxis here," he said, directing the boys to an old-model car. After their bags were put in the boot, the four climbed in. "We go to the company store first," Caron directed the driver.

Presently they pulled up in front of a well-built wooden structure near the edge of town. A large sign over the entrance said: *Hudson's Bay Company*.

"What do you know!" Chet said, as they pushed open the door. "It looks like a department store in Bayport."

The large interior was filled with tables displaying brightly coloured, heavy woollen clothing. A variety of rifles and leather goods hung on the walls. There were only a few other people in the store, and Caribou Caron led the way straight to a counter at the back.

"There's the factor," the trapper said.

"The what?" Chet asked.

Caribou explained that the factor was the man who ran the store for the Hudson's Bay Company. The trapper strode over to a husky man, whom he introduced to the boys as Bill Stone. They all shook hands.

Frank asked, "Do you remember a man who bought ten drums of aviation fuel and two drums of oil the other day?"

"Sure, I remember him," the man said. "He gave me new hundred-dollar bills."

"*Bon tonnerre!*" Caribou shouted. "Monsieur Baker-Jones paid me for the rune stone in new hundred-dollar bills. That man who buy fuel and oil is the bandit who robbed us!"

"It does look like it," Frank said slowly, "though it

could be coincidence. Don't forget, there must be some other new hundred-dollar bills around."

"*Oui*, I know!" Caribou was excited. "But I feel this is our man—one of the thieves."

"Did he give his name?" Joe asked Bill Stone.

Before the store manager had a chance to answer, something whizzed past Frank's head. *Thunk!* A steel knife blade embedded itself in the wall behind him. It hung there, quivering.

"Yowee!" Frank gasped, jumping back. The knife had almost grazed his hair.

"*Bon tonnerre!*" yelled Caribou, whirling around.

The French-Canadian had instinctively crouched like a panther about to attack. He was ready for action, and his eyes flickered as he glanced in all directions.

There was no one in sight!

The shock of the attack over, there was a mad dash to the open door. Outside, the boys and the French-Canadian scanned the street. The few passers-by looked harmless enough, and none could recall seeing a fleeing man.

"A clean getaway," Joe said glumly.

"*Sacre bleu!*" Caribou exploded.

"That sure was no accident," Frank said grimly, regaining his usual calm. "We must really have hit the trail of something big."

The group walked back into the store, where Mr Stone stood looking out of the window. "Did you find the knife thrower?" he asked worriedly.

"No!" Caribou boomed. "But we will!"

"Maybe it was the person who bought the aviation fuel," Chet guessed.

"It could have been," Frank agreed. He put the knife into his pocket, then asked the manager, "What is the name of the fuel customer?"

"He told me he was Jesse Keating," Stone answered.

"An alias, probably," said Frank, after hearing a description of the purchaser. "I'll bet he was Kelly."

"Did he say where he was going?" Joe asked.

"Yes. To tow the fuel down Slave River on a raft to a lumber camp."

"Lumber camp?" Caribou raised his eyebrows. "There is no lumber camp between here and Great Slave Lake."

"Say, that's right, Caribou!" said the manager, scratching his head. "Wonder where he *was* heading?"

"I have a hunch maybe he was taking the gas to a hideout where he'll fuel that stolen float plane," Frank said thoughtfully. "Now we have to figure out where the hideout is. Have you a map we could look at, Mr Stone?"

"Sure," the grey-haired man replied. "Here's a good one. Keep it!"

The boys crowded round the detailed map of the area. "This is where we are," Caribou pointed out. "And this is the Wood Buffalo Park."

"That would be a great place for a hideout," Joe said. "Is it open to everyone, Caribou?"

"Yes, but you must have a permit," the trapper answered. "The office is down the street."

"Let's see who else has applied for a permit recently," Frank suggested. "Maybe Keating is taking cover in the park."

Everyone agreed. Mr Stone said the travellers were

welcome to leave their luggage as long as necessary. Outside, Frank suggested they first report the knife-throwing incident to the Mounted Police. The group went directly to the station, and handed the weapon to the officer in charge.

"We'll do everything possible to have the owner traced," the Mountie promised.

Next, Caribou accompanied the boys to the Wood Buffalo Park office. A bald man of about thirty, dressed in a khaki shirt and shorts, greeted them as they entered the small wooden building. "Caribou, I thought you were going to stay in the city and be a dude!" He grinned at the bearded trapper, who laughed loudly.

Caribou introduced the man as Curly Pike, assistant superintendent of the buffalo preserve. As the boys smiled over the humorous misnomer, Caribou said that Curly, as well as his boss, Superintendent Breen Connor could fly anything with wings.

Frank asked Curly Pike if any strangers had entered the buffalo park recently. He explained about Jesse Keating and his cargo of fuel drums.

"We haven't issued any permits to a stranger for the past two weeks," Curly replied, looking at the duplicates of the pass applications.

"Could a man have entered the park illegally?" Joe queried.

Curly Pike rubbed the top of his bald head thoughtfully. "It's possible. That's mighty rugged country and difficult to patrol. Somebody could sneak in without being seen."

Disappointed, the boys thanked Curly, who wished

them luck in their search. "Sorry not to be of any help," he called, as they went out the door.

"We can still go on a search downriver," Joe urged.

"It sounds funny to say 'down' a river which runs north," Chet said. "The current will help us, too!"

"We'll need a canoe," Caribou said, heading down the main street of Fort Smith. "Come!"

When they reached the small docks at the edge of the river landing, Caribou made arrangements to hire a canoe with an outboard motor. He told the boatyard owner that they would be back for the craft in about two hours.

"What about food?" Chet pleaded. "We can't go without that."

Frank and Joe laughed at their chubby friend. "That's a good suggestion," Joe added.

"We'll go for supplies while our canoe's being fuelled," Frank said. "I've ordered some extra tanks of petrol put aboard."

The group trudged back up the hill to the Hudson's Bay store to buy tinned meats, dried fruits and vegetables, and some new lines for their fishing rods.

After a snack the group went back to the supply store and picked up their provisions. Mr Stone offered to keep their suitcases for the duration of the river trip and to accept messages for them. They took what clothing they would need from their bags, and went down to the dock. The boys stowed the rucksacks of food and clothes in the canoe, a large aluminium one with three paddles. Then they started down the Slave River, with Caribou in the stern handling the rudder and motor controls.

Skilfully he guided the craft past the dangerous upjutting rocks and swirling currents. Soon they were out of sight of Fort Smith.

"This looks like pioneer country, all right," Joe observed presently.

When they rounded a bend, Caribou pointed out white water in the broad river. "Arctic wind is kicking up trouble," he commented. Even as he spoke, the canoe began to pitch on the choppy surface.

The stream grew suddenly rougher, and the light-weight craft rocked from side to side.

"*Tonnerre!*" Caribou boomed over the sound of the wind. "Hang on!"

The boys gripped the edges of the canoe to steady themselves as it heaved up and down in the growing swell. Chet, who was seated in the bow, gasped and exclaimed, "We've sprung a leak!"

· 8 ·

Missing Campers

"WE are sinking!" shouted Caribou. "To shore!" Just then there was a sputter as the outboard motor conked out. "*Sacre bleu!*" the French-Canadian yelled.

Frank and Joe grabbed paddles while Chet tore off his shirt and used it to plug the hole in the canoe. The Hardys paddled furiously while Caribou pulled at the motor's starting rope. The outboard coughed once, but did not turn over.

"Engine's probably flooded from spray," Joe panted. "What luck!"

Caribou also seized a paddle and his strong back muscles flexed as he strained to help turn the rocking boat towards shore.

Frank felt as though his aching arms would break. Perspiration glistened on his and Joe's foreheads. In spite of Chet's efforts to plug the leak, the water poured in.

"Paddle!" shouted Caribou. "Faster, boys, faster!"

Frank and Joe put greater effort into their strokes. The heavily laden canoe pushed and ploughed its way through the waves, and as the bow neared shore, suddenly touched bottom. Chet leaped out into knee-deep water. Frank, Joe, and Caribou followed. Grabbing the sides of the boat, they hauled it up over the rocks on to a small beach.

Exhausted, the foursome dropped to the sand to rest. As soon as Joe had caught his breath he said disgustedly, "We'll have a hard time finding the thieves now!"

"*Bon tonnerre!*" Caribou shouted, leaping to his feet. "We must unload gear before she gets wet!"

"And how!" Chet cried as the boys jumped up. "Rescue the food!"

With the four working quickly, the canoe was emptied and turned over. The Hardys then examined the bottom of the metal craft.

"Hey!" Frank cried out. "Look! This leak was caused deliberately!"

Everyone crowded round to look. Very cleverly five of the rivets that held the aluminium sides to the keel had been taken out and replaced with bits of putty.

"Pretty foxy—whoever did it," said Joe, sitting back on his heels. "The putty would be waterproof and hold tight until strain was put on the hull."

"If we hadn't moved fast," Chet put in, "we'd be swimming right now."

"*Tonnerre!*" Caribou shouted. "That rascal nearly succeed this time. But no more!"

"You mean your friend Dulac?" Frank asked. "Or one of the thieves?"

The trapper shrugged, and Joe said, "It's anybody's guess. But whoever did it must have sneaked into the boatyard and tampered with the canoe while we were gone."

"I think I can make repairs," Caribou said, and went to work quickly, using bits of bent wire. Finally the craft was placed back in the water and proved seaworthy.

After cleaning and refuelling the outboard motor, the boys and their guide set out again down the river. It was growing dusky.

"We'll have to stop for the night soon," Caribou advised.

They cruised along smoothly and after a time spotted a canoe coming upstream. In the craft sat two men in khakis.

"Hunters," said Caribou.

"Let's ask them if they've seen a raft with petrol drums aboard," Frank suggested, and hailed the men.

The wind had died down, so the two canoes now lay quietly side by side. Caribou questioned the hunters, since they spoke only French.

There was a rapid-fire discussion among the three. After a few minutes Caribou pushed the other boat and waved as the strangers continued their trip upstream.

"They have come right from the mouth of the river," he reported. "They saw no boat towing a raft."

Frank frowned. "The thief may have reached the float plane already or pulled into hiding along the shore if he spotted those men."

"That is right," Caribou agreed. "But now it is too dark to look for him. Ahead I see a good camping place for us."

A few minutes later the searchers entered a small cove with a smooth beach. The boys hopped out, and slid the canoe carefully up a gently shelving rock. After unloading the supplies, they carried the craft on to the beach and placed it on props.

Frank took a lightweight axe from the pack and began gathering firewood. Joe went down to the bank to catch fish for supper, while Chet spread reindeer moss, which he covered with balsam tips for a sleeping area. He rolled out the boys' sleeping bags on to this cushioning.

Caribou sat down on a rock and watched as the three boys worked rapidly and efficiently. "You are good campers," he said, obviously impressed.

The fire was hot when Joe returned with a half dozen grayling. The fish were quickly fried, and the hungry travellers ate them with canned stewed tomatoes and brown bread. After they had finished the meal and cleaned the cooking utensils, Joe put another log on the fire and the four sat back, relaxed.

"Why are you called Caribou?" Frank asked the trapper.

Caribou said that when he was a small boy, he had come to this territory from the Ungava district near Labrador. "No caribou there. I was very smart." He grinned widely. "The first time I see one, I think it is cow!" He spoke in his old patois.

"Trapper tell me to pet the cow, so I walk up to the big caribou. I get a surprise. She turn quick and rush at me. I run fast, just make it to tree, but her horns tear my pants."

The three boys laughed heartily and Chet said, "Moo! Some cow!"

"After that," said Caribou, "all the trappers in the north country call me Caribou Caron."

The burly man regaled his young companions with several hair-raising stories of his life in the north. Then they all crawled into their sleeping bags and were soon in deep slumber.

Joe did not know how long he had been alseep when he heard a *crack* loud enough to make him sit up and listen intently.

The fire had died down and the air was still. He glanced around the campfire. Caribou and Chet were not there!

Joe, alarmed, shook his brother awake. Frank rolled over drowsily and asked, "Wh-a-at's wrong?"

"Caribou and Chet have gone," Joe told him.

Frank became fully awake now. "Gone?" he echoed. "Where?"

"I don't know. Something must have awakened them," Joe answered, "and they went to investigate."

The Hardys threw more wood on the fire to light up the area. As the chips flared up brightly, they began a search of the campsite. Suddenly, from the far side of the fire, came a "*Sh!*"

The Hardys swung round. Out of the shadows stepped a medium-sized, roughly dressed man. He was wiry and tough looking.

"Who are you?" Frank demanded. "What are you doing here?"

The man attempted a weak smile, then said, "My name is Soleau, and I've come to warn you about your guide, Caribou Caron."

"What about Caribou?" Joe asked. He instinctively did not like the man.

"Caron is dangerous—mentally unbalanced," the stranger said. "And he's leading you on a wild goose chase."

"Where is Caribou now?" Frank asked warily.

"He has taken your friend as a hostage," Soleau said with a sneer.

"A hostage!" Joe repeated. "I don't believe you!"

"It's true," the stranger insisted, edging his way closer to Frank. "You fellows had better go back to Fort Smith or you'll be next."

"Look out!" Joe yelled suddenly. But he was too late. *Bam!* Soleau swung a powerful right punch at Frank. The boy had no time to duck as the rock-like fist cracked against his jaw.

As Frank dropped unconscious by the fire, Joe leaped across the flames at Soleau. With a crashing tackle Joe brought him down. The stranger's feet came up in a vicious kick and knocked the wind out of the boy. Shaking his head and gasping for breath, Joe reached around the man's neck and hung on. The two rolled on the ground, coming dangerously close to the red-hot coals of the campfire. The top of Joe's head grew hot as Soleau forced him nearer and nearer the flames.

Suddenly from the darkness came a great roar. "*Bon tonnerre!*" Caribou crashed through the brush, slashing at branches with his mighty arms. Behind him was Chet.

Caribou crossed the fire in a leap. Grasping the stranger by the shoulders, he pulled him off Joe and flung him away. Soleau flew through the air, arms and legs waving wildly.

But the wiry man knew how to fall. As his weight hit the ground, he rolled quickly to his feet and disappeared in the darkness.

"After him!" Chet cried.

"No!" boomed Caribou. "We never find him in the dark. Help Frank!"

Chet came back to his friend, and Joe scrambled up to assist.

Frank roused when the boys put cold water on his head, and he sat up groggily. "Wow, did he pack a punch!" he said.

"That was Abner Dulac," Caron snorted in disgust. "A dangerous fox!"

"What's he got against us?" Frank asked, touching his jaw gingerly.

"Anybody who is a friend of mine is an enemy of Dulac," Caribou answered. "It was that lowdown weasel all the time!"

The Hardys looked puzzled and Chet explained. "I heard a noise like a bear prowling and woke up Caribou. We followed the sound for a while. It led away from the camp. Dulac must have circled back to steal our gear."

"Why?" asked Joe in surprise.

Caribou smiled wryly. "One reason, Dulac will take anything. He is a thief. Up here in the north, you die if you have no gear!"

Joe grimaced. "Great mackerel! You mean he'd let us die!"

Caribou nodded solemnly. "I warned you—that Dulac is a mean one! He would stop short at nothing. He cares for no-one but himself."

Chet looked apprehensive. "Do you think he'll keep on our trail and cause us more trouble?"

The big trapper shrugged. "It could be so. Who can tell with a man like Dulac? We will have to keep eyes in the backs of our heads."

Frank had been silent, mulling over the recent incident. Now he said, "What I can't figure out is *why* Dulac went to all the trouble of following us here—even using a phoney name to trick us. He must be up to something more serious than robbing traps—or trying to spite you, Caribou."

The others agreed. "But what?" Joe said in a puzzled voice.

"No more mysteries tonight!" Chet begged. "I've had enough. My head's sore trying to puzzle all this out. How about a little sleep?"

The boys and Caribou were soon back in their bags. They dozed off but their rest was fitful. The recent events were preying on their minds.

The next morning was bright and clear. After washing in the bracing river, the group had a good breakfast. Everyone pitched in to break camp, then they set out in the canoe again.

As the sun grew hotter, hordes of insects began to buzz about the boys' heads, and they quickly covered their upper bodies with the netting they had brought along.

"Dad was right about these pests!" Joe said, slapping at a persistent black fly. "Thank goodness we've got the nets. We'd be eaten alive!"

During the next four hours, they navigated down the rapidly moving river, searching for the petrol raft. They were perspiring from the heat and were growing discouraged when Frank suddenly pointed to the shore.

"Over there!" he called out.

A crude log raft was barely visible under low-hanging brush. Quickly Caribou stopped the engine, and the boys paddled swiftly to shore.

Joe jumped out first and ran to the raft. Reaching it, he called excitedly, "We've found it! I can smell petrol!"

· 9 ·

Grizzly Charge!

EXCITED but silent, Frank and Chet slipped out of the canoe, and with Caribou's help, hauled the boat up on the beach. They rushed over to join Joe at the raft.

"*Bon tonnerre!*" The French-Canadian trapper gave a huge sniff. "This certainly carry fuel!"

"We can't be sure that this is Keating's raft," Chet spoke up.

"No," said Frank. "But it's a good place to start a search and find the owner's identity. Let's separate and look for a trail."

The four spread out in different directions, struggling through the dense, tangled undergrowth back from the river. Suddenly Frank gave a birdcall from a thicket to signal the others.

"I've found an opening!" he told them. "Over here!" His companions joined him quickly and found Frank at the head of a crude, narrow trail. He and Joe dropped to their knees and studied the path and the weeds at the edge.

The boys noted that the dirt bore scrape marks and the growth was trampled. Frank announced triumphantly, "Something heavy was dragged or rolled along

73

here not too long ago—and, from the footprints, probably by two men."

"Like a fuel drum?" Joe added, grinning.

"Ah!" Caribou exclaimed, his eyes flashing. "Come on! We'll follow their trail!"

He and the boys rushed back to the canoe and unloaded their gear. They strapped on their rucksacks. Chet and Caribou took the rest of the equipment, while Frank and Joe carried the canoe.

The searchers set forth on the trail. For the first hundred yards it was narrow and roughly blazed. The group trudged along as the path twisted and turned, growing wider as they walked farther inland. Finally the trail led up the face of a rugged incline.

"Whew! That'll be a tough haul," Joe said, as they all paused to rest.

The Hardys decided to leave the supplies and canoe camouflaged beneath some dense brush. Then the ascent began.

"Boy!" Chet puffed. "Lucky we left our stuff back there and didn't lug it!"

"*Oui*," said Caribou. "The men with the drum were very determined."

Frank was first to reach the top. He found himself gazing out over a small, sparkling, jewel-like lake about a mile in diameter. The shores were ringed with tall, stately Canadian blue spruce trees.

The other three scrambled to join him at the summit. "Pretty nice," said Joe. "I could go for a dive in there." He mopped his brow.

"Me, too," Chet added emphatically.

The four hurried along the trail, which was smooth

and well cleared, to the edge of the small lake. There the drag marks disappeared into the water. But there was nothing in sight on the smooth surface.

"Let's circle the lake," Frank suggested, and they tramped along the curving shore.

About a quarter of the way round, Joe suddenly pointed offshore. "What's that out there?" he asked excitedly.

Everyone stared at a floating object glinting in the sunlight on the surface of the lake.

"It's an empty fuel drum!" said Frank.

"What a clue!" Chet exclaimed.

The boys stripped to their pants, swam out, retrieved the metal cylinder, and dragged it up on to the sandy beach.

Caribou rolled the drum over for inspection. "It's Keating's all right," he announced, pointing to the Hudson's Bay stencil 42. "This is the Fort Smith store number."

"The petrol probably was used to fuel a plane," Frank surmised.

"The stolen float plane, I'll bet!" Joe said elatedly. "Hey! This lake would be a swell landing spot—the crooks' hideout could be right near here!"

"Or," Chet put in, "the fuel could have been flown to another spot."

"We look around," Caribou said.

They started to circle the shore again, fanning out a hundred yards apart. Frank and Joe converged in a grassy meadow when suddenly they heard rustling in a clump of shrubs ahead.

Stalking silently through the grass, they approached

the bushes. The rustling grew louder. The brothers were about to push aside the shrubbery when Frank put his hand on Joe's arm, restraining him.

"*Good grief!*" Joe gasped.

Several yards to their right was a huge brown grizzly bear! Beside her were two small furry cubs. The Hardys stood as if frozen, hoping that the bear had not seen them. The mother bear growled, and reared up to her full six-feet height, standing upright. Her enormous head was ferocious looking, with her jaws held open and the small ears laid back flat.

Frank took one second to notice that the beast's long sharp claws were extended. "Head for the woods!" he hissed, pushing Joe in front of him.

The brothers raced off for their lives. The huge bear dropped to four legs. Though awkward and lumbering, she proved terrifyingly fast as she charged after the Hardys.

Suddenly Caribou came crashing through the bushes. The giant trapper held his hat in one hand and a large plaid handkerchief in the other. He waved them frantically, and kept shouting, "Hey! Hey!" at the top of his lungs.

The bear's charge faltered as she became aware of Caribou's actions. The huge creature swerved to her right and started to lumber in the direction of the French-Canadian. "Get up a tree, fast!" he yelled to Frank and Joe. "Go on!"

The Hardys obeyed and shinned up the nearest trees. They clambered on to stout limbs and sat gasping for breath.

Caribou raced off in another direction and climbed

up a low branched spruce. The mother bear padded over and began to sniff around the trunk of the tree where the trapper was perched. Suddenly there was a squeal from one of the cubs. Ears perked up, the grizzly stood still, listening. The cub squealed again. This time the mother turned and trotted back to her offspring.

"Whew!" said Joe in a low voice.

"That was close!" Frank whispered, expelling his breath sharply.

The brothers remained in the trees until they saw the bear and her cubs move off in the opposite direction towards the lake.

Frank and Joe quickly dropped to the ground. Caribou had already climbed down from the spruce and hurried to meet them. He had a wide grin on his face.

"Plenty of excitement in my country, no?"

"Plenty is right!" Joe exclaimed. "Grizzlies I can do without, though!"

The Hardys thanked the veteran trapper for coming to their rescue. Caribou explained that as a rule bears are not troublesome when they have cubs.

"Unless you get too close," he said. "Then the mother will charge to protect her young. The best way to escape is to distract her and climb a tree. Grizzlies don't climb."

Just then Chet came running up, out of breath. "What happened?" he demanded.

Upon hearing of the adventure, Chet shuddered at his friends' narrow escape. "I'd rather be surrounded by thieves than tangle with one of those beasts!"

"Let's stop for lunch now," Caribou suggested.

"That's a good idea," Frank agreed. "Running away from bears makes me hungry."

The trekkers dug into their rucksacks and soon were enjoying tinned-meat sandwiches and tomato juice. Then, keeping a sharp lookout for more bears, the group continued their search around the lake.

"No signs of any habitation around here," Joe observed to his brother.

At that moment Chet, who was a little distance ahead, beckoned to the others. When they reached him, he pointed out broad imprints in the sandy beach.

"Looks as if heavy objects were dragged across," Frank noted.

"This is where the other drums were pulled out of the water!" Joe cried out.

"Look at this!" Frank stooped to pick up a short metal object. "A wrench," he said, turning it over in his hand. "'Yellowknife Lodge' has been stencilled on to the handle." He handed the tool to Caribou.

"The lodge is on north shore of Great Slave Lake," Caribou said. "Long distance away. This may belong to hunters stopping there."

Frank had another theory. "Or maybe the wrench was dropped by the man called Keating who brought the fuel drums here!"

"If so, he must be one of the gang that's been robbing lodges in that area," Joe deduced. "Wonder if Biff, Tony, and Sam are having any luck on the case."

"We'll hang on to this wrench for evidence," Frank said, and put the tool in his pocket.

"*S-s-sh!*" Caribou broke in, holding up his hand and cocking his head to one side, listening.

"A plane," Joe whispered as the droning noise became louder. "We've been spotted!"

Everyone stood tensely, staring at the small float plane which came into sight. Who was aboard—the thieves? The plane touched its pontoons on to the lake surface and taxied over to the group on shore.

"Look!" Chet exclaimed. "What's that big bright marking on the door?"

"*Bon tonnerre!*" Caribou burst out. "They are not robbers! The crest on the door is for Royal Canadian Mounted Police!"

"The Mounties!" Chet smiled in relief as the craft ran up on to the beach.

The engine was cut. A thin, uniformed man opened the cockpit door and jumped to the ground.

"I'm looking for Frank and Joe Hardy," the Mountie said in a serious tone of voice.

·10·

An Amazing Suspect

"I'M Frank Hardy, and this is my brother, Joe," Frank told the Mountie. "Why do you want us?"

"And how did you locate us?" Chet queried.

The pilot pulled out his wallet and showed his identification card. "I'm Corporal Fergus of the Fort Smith station," he said. "I have an urgent message for you, so I flew downriver. From two thousand feet up I spotted you walking along the beach."

"Has anything happened to our family?" Joe asked the officer quickly.

"No. The message concerns the man impersonating your father," Corporal Fergus replied. "The Edmonton police have been notified that someone else called to see Mr Baker-Jones at the hospital. It's thought he may be an accomplice of the impostor because Mr Baker-Jones doesn't know anyone around here."

Frank queried, "Do the police know his identity?"

"They have investigated the Edmonton hotels," said the officer, "and learned that a man of his description is registered in one as 'J. C. Phillips.' Right now they are keeping a close watch on the hotel and plan to follow the man as soon as he's spotted."

"Two of us should be there," Frank said seriously.

"Joe, you and Chet go back to Edmonton. Caribou and I will continue our search for the thieves up here."

"Fine," his brother agreed. "We'll meet you back at Fort Smith in a couple of days."

"Maybe your dad's impersonator will lead us to the stolen rune stone!" Chet said.

"That's possible," Joe agreed. "Could be the stone wasn't brought up here after all. Anyhow, we'll have both places covered."

Chet looked worried. "Say, how do we get back to Edmonton?"

Corporal Fergus stepped forward. "I'm to fly you to Fort Smith," he said. "From there, you can get a plane to Edmonton."

"Swell! Thanks a million," Joe said.

Caribou spoke up. "Meantime, Frank and I will return to Fort Smith. We will look for thieves on the way. And travel most of the night."

Frank had a new idea. "When we get there, let's hire a float plane and start a search from the air, Caribou. We might sight the stolen aircraft."

The Mountie shook his head sceptically. "In this area that will be like looking for a needle in a haystack! We're working on the case, too, without much luck."

"If I know my brother," Joe said, grinning, "he'll find the plane if it's around."

Joe and Chet said goodbye to Frank and Caribou, and climbed into the RCMP float plane. The two on shore watched and waved as the sleek craft turned and taxied off over the small lake. The water sprayed in tall sheets as the pontoons lifted and the plane took off, just clearing the tops of the spruce trees rimming the water.

Frank and Caribou retraced their steps to the canoe. They carried the craft and other equipment back to Slave River and were soon headed for Fort Smith.

Meanwhile, in the RCMP plane, Corporal Fergus pointed out the densely forested land and the snakelike outline of Slave River below.

When they approached the Fort Smith airfield, the afternoon flight to Edmonton was in the process of loading. Corporal Fergus called over the roar of the motor, "We have to land in the river, but I'll ask the tower by radio to hold the plane for you."

The control tower agreed, and after setting down, the boys took time to thank Corporal Fergus before they climbed out of the plane which had taxied to the airfield dock.

"Lots of luck," the corporal called out to them.

"Maybe we'll see you later," said Joe as he and Chet waved goodbye.

Soon the two boys had boarded the waiting plane, which took off seconds later. The trip was fast and smooth and the boys landed at Edmonton rested and ready for more work.

The taxi journey from the airport in to town was long and slow through heavy traffic. Joe shifted impatiently in his seat. "I hope we get there before they question that man," he said. "I'd like to be on hand for the surprise!"

When they finally pulled up in front of the Edmonton police headquarters, Inspector Knight was just coming out of the front door.

"Hello, boys! Glad you're here," he said, smiling warmly and extending his hand. "We're going over to the hospital. Our men report that the suspect is heading there."

Joe was surprised. "You haven't picked him up yet?" he asked.

"The fellow really hasn't *done* anything," the inspector replied. "But if he goes to the hospital to see Baker-Jones again, we'll question him."

Joe and Chet drove off in a police car with Inspector Knight and another officer, who was at the wheel. When they reached the hospital, the driver parked at the side entrance.

"We'll sit here and keep watch," said the inspector.

Ten minutes later he exclaimed, "There he is!"

Inspector Knight indicated a man coming down the street towards the front of the hospital. He had bushy black hair and a moustache, and, the boys noticed, was walking with a distinct limp. He went slowly up the steps to the building and into the entrance hall.

Both officers and the two boys slipped from the car and followed quietly. Inside, they saw the stranger go directly to the reception desk and heard him ask to see Mr Baker-Jones.

"Your name, please?" the man asked politely.

"Phillips."

Instantly the inspector went forward. "We'd like to ask you a few questions, Mr Phillips," he said.

The stranger swung round quickly. Suddenly Joe gasped. Then he dashed up to the man and stood, stockstill, staring at him. The bushy-haired caller straightened up and smiled.

"Joe! Chet!" he said in a familiar voice.

Chet's mouth flew open. "Wh-a-at! Mr Hardy!" He gaped. "Boy oh boy! You had *me* fooled!"

"But not Joe," the detective said.

"What does this mean?" Inspector Knight asked, greatly perplexed.

Moving away from the reception desk, Mr Hardy stripped off his moustache and wig. He introduced himself quickly to the Canadian police officer, then explained, "I thought I would be able to foil the rune stone crooks by coming up here in disguise—make them think I was still in Bayport." He chuckled. "I didn't figure on getting caught by my own son!"

"I'm sorry, Dad," Joe said. "Guess maybe I spoiled your plan."

"I doubt it," Mr Hardy said, putting an arm round his son's shoulders. "You boys were really on the alert—I'm proud of you!"

He turned to Inspector Knight. "As long as we're both here, perhaps we can compare notes on this case."

"Fine, Mr Hardy," said the inspector. "I've wanted to meet you for a long time. Only I'm afraid my department hasn't turned up any new leads to that impostor or to the stolen stone and money."

"How is Mr Baker-Jones?" Joe asked.

"The hospital told me this morning," Inspector Knight replied, "that he is improving, but still in no condition to answer questions."

"Well, we'll keep working on the case," Mr Hardy promised.

The Bayport group said goodbye to the officers, then went back to the detective's hotel room for a conference.

Joe told his father about the knife thrower and gave

him details of the Fort Smith and Slave River trip. He explained where Frank and Caribou were and about their continuing hunt for the stolen float plane. Mr Hardy was expecially interested to hear that they had found one of the petrol drums and a wrench from Yellowknife Lodge.

Joe asked, "Dad, have you had any more news from Sam Radley?"

"Yes," replied the detective. "Just before I left home I had a report. Sam thinks the lodge thefts gang is still operating around Great Slave Lake. He, Biff, and Tony have traced them as far as the town of Snowdrift. That's the last I've heard."

Joe looked thoughtful. "Dad," he said, "I have a hunch there might be another motive behind these lodge thefts besides burglary. The gang might be using the stolen float plane for some other purpose."

"You have a point there, Joe," his father agreed. "Finding the plane would be a big step in cracking the case."

"We'll get back to Fort Smith as early as possible tomorrow," Joe proposed, "and help Frank and Caribou search by air."

"Good," said the detective. "I'll remain here in case I can speak with Mr Baker-Jones."

Chet offered to make reservations for a morning flight. This done, the three showered, then had a juicy steak dinner.

Afterwards, Joe sent a telegram to the Hudson's Bay Company store at Fort Smith telling Frank that he and Chet would be there by the following midday. After a quick breakfast the following morning, Joe and Chet took the plane back to Fort Smith. When they landed, Frank and Caribou were waiting at the airport to greet them.

"What's new?" Frank asked.

"Our dad has changed his name," said Joe, grinning, and told the story.

Frank laughed heartily.

"I've arranged to hire a float plane," he said. "It's moored at a dock on the river."

"Today," Caribou boomed, "our luck will be better! We search by air for the stolen plane."

Shortly afterwards, with Frank at the controls, the foursome took off. Soon they were clear of the airfield and circling over and away from the town of Fort Smith. "We'll fly a box search, south of Great Slave Lake and west of Snowdrift," Frank announced. "Keep your eyes open for any sign of the stolen plane."

The four were silent as they peered intently out of the windows. They flew for an hour in the planned pattern. Not one of the searchers spotted the slightest clue to the missing craft.

"*Bon tonnerre!*" Caribou burst out finally. "These woods are too thick to see into!"

The plane droned on, over one small lake after another. Chet's head was nodding sleepily when Joe sat up sharply and called out, "I see something!" He pointed to an L-shaped body of water. "There's the plane!"

"*Sacre bleu!*" Caribou thundered. "We find it! I told you our luck would be better."

The young pilot banked the light plane around and

they went down low, retracing their course over the lake. The craft Joe had sighted was resting in the middle of the water. The trees at the edge of the lake were tall and the undergrowth thick.

"It's going to be tricky to land down there," Frank said, circling again. "But here goes!"

He slowed the engine enough to sideslip over the high trees and on the surface of the lake. As they straightened out for the downwind leg of the approach, Joe suddenly shouted to Frank.

"It's just an old wreck! One of the wings is in the water!"

"We're already committed to this landing," Frank told him. "We'll have to go ahead. Keep your fingers crossed." The plane continued to drop into the landing position. Frank lowered the rudder and started pulling the throttle back.

Suddenly Caribou shouted in alarm, "Watch out! Logs!"

Directly beyond and just under the surface of the water, they could see a twisted tangle of rough logs. The float plane was heading right for them! Would they manage to avoid certain disaster?

For a moment everyone stared ahead. Then Frank jammed the throttle forward, and eased back on the stick gradually.

"I must be careful. I mustn't rush it. Too much lift will throw us into a stall," he told himself, determined not to panic.

From behind came Chet's frantic cry. "The trees! Watch the trees!"

Frank's brow glistened with perspiration as he

manipulated the stick gently. The dark woods loomed up ahead of them as their old plane climbed slowly. The boys gritted their teeth and Caribou clenched his seat belt until his knuckles grew white.

The plane seemed to be barely rising. Would they gain altitude in time to avoid a crash?

· 11 ·

Surprise Tactics

"Hang on!" Frank shouted, holding the throttle hard ahead.

The plane banked sharply on its side. As the towering black-green spruce trees loomed up at them, the three passengers braced themselves for a collision.

But the old craft responded instantly and slipped across the trees, riding on the left wing. The boys could hear the boughs scrape the underside of the plane. The floats jerked as they were caught momentarily, then released by the tree-tops.

Frank righted the plane, pulling back hard on the stick. The craft was in the clear!

"Whew!" He let out his breath slowly, blinking as his taut nerves relaxed. "That was a tight one!" He could hear sighs of relief from his companions.

Joe leaned forward in his seat and gripped Frank's shoulder. "Pretty fancy flying, brother!" he said, and Chet and Caribou added their praise.

"It was a good workout," Frank said modestly. "Now back to the search."

He circled the aircraft over the lake again, staying higher this time. Grimly Joe pointed to the submerged logs on each side of the wrecked plane. They were roped together.

"Those logs were put there deliberately," he said. "Someone went to a lot of trouble to booby-trap us!"

"The thieves know we hunt for them," Caribou muttered. "We must be very careful!"

The plane cruised over the lake and wooded area again. There was no one in sight, nor was there any trace of a plane.

"Wonder where the gang found that wreck?" Joe mused.

"It could have been abandoned somewhere in these woods," Frank suggested. "And they dragged it out on to the lake."

"That would have been a tough job," Chet remarked.

"Let's get back to Forth Smith and report this to the Mounties," Frank suggested. "Maybe they know something about it."

The others agreed, and they headed back to town. As they approached the landing, Frank radioed ahead for clearance. When he set down he taxied straight to the RCMP jetty. They went at once to the office. Corporal Fergus was there and listened intently to their story.

"Could that abandoned plane have been found in the woods, Corporal?" asked Frank.

"One *was* wrecked up there in the bush some time ago," Fergus replied. "Whoever dragged it out to the lake must know the area well."

"Why?" Chet asked.

"Not too many people were familiar with the location of that wreck," the corporal answered.

"Would Abner Dulac be familiar with that territory, Caribou?" Frank asked suddenly.

"*Oui*." Caribou nodded. "That Dulac run his traplines through there many times."

"I've been trying to figure out why Dulac trailed us from Edmonton," Frank said. "One reason could be he's mixed up with the rune stone theft."

"Sounds possible," Joe agreed. "And he either was on his way to warn his buddies about us, or wanted to stop our sleuthing cold—or both."

"He is a snake. He would do it," Caribou declared angrily.

Corporal Fergus said he would send several Mounted Police up to the area of the abandoned plane to look around. If they reported anything suspicious, he would let the Hardys know.

When the brothers and their friends started back along the jetty towards their craft, Joe suddenly stopped. "There's a guy nosing round our plane."

Quickly the three boys ran down the jetty. By now the fellow was leaning over, the upper half of his body inside the plane. Frank grasped him by the arm and pulled him up.

"Biff!" he shouted in surprise. "Boy, it's good to see you. But what are you doing here?"

"Looking for you," the lanky boy replied, grinning. "Your father cabled Sam, telling us where to reach you." He added that Tony and Radley were in the town of Hay River.

After Caribou joined them and introductions were made, Biff explained, "We tracked the gang to Hay River—west of the mouth of Slave River. But they're plenty shrewd at eluding us. So Sam wants you all to come up and join forces with us. I came in on the early-morning plane."

The Hardys and Chet then brought Biff up to date on their own experiences and detective work—both on the Viking rune stone mystery and the lodge thefts case.

"I hate to give up the search for Keating and his fuel drums," Frank concluded. "And I'd like to find out if Abner Dulac *is* mixed up with the thieves."

"Me, too!" Caribou put in hotly. "You boys go to Hay River. I will stay here and watch for Dulac."

"All right, Caribou," Frank agreed, smiling at the trapper. "You can have first crack at your friend Dulac!"

"*Bon tonnerre!*" Caribou exploded. "Friend, never!"

After the boys had attended to having the hired plane fuelled and inspected, they had lunch, then bid goodbye to the French-Canadian. Joe slid into the pilot's seat, and with Frank, Chet, and Biff as passengers, taxied out on to the river. The take-off was smooth and rapid and soon the plane was heading out over the dense spruce forest on the northwestern route to the town of Hay River.

When they came in sight of the town, Joe landed the float plane and tied up at an airfield jetty. The four jumped out and Biff led them down the main street to a small, old hotel where Sam Radley and Tony were waiting.

"Hi! Swell to see you!" they were greeted excitedly. Sam Radley, a man of medium height, wiry build, and thinning sandy hair, shook their hands.

The groups exchanged accounts of their recent activities on the mysteries.

"There's no doubt," said Sam, "that the gang we're after has some thoroughly experienced woodsmen."

"We feel they're close by," added Tony, "and so do the Mounties."

"The thieves' operations seem to centre around lodges on the shore of Great Slave Lake," Sam continued. "So far, they've never stolen from places inland."

Frank said thoughtfully, "It could be coincidence of course— but the locale of these lodge thefts and the finding of the Viking rune stone is the same—Great Slave Lake."

Joe threw his brother a keen glance. "In other words, you think it *isn't* coincidence—that there's a connection between the two mysteries."

"Yes," Frank replied with conviction. "For two reasons: our radio antenna was knocked down while Dad was receiving your report on the lodge thefts, Sam. Kelly could have been eavesdropping outside. And," he went on, "Kelly is also a suspect in the missing rune stone case."

Joe broke in. "That means those new hundred-dollar bills stolen from Caribou and the ones used to pay for the fuel drums in Fort Smith are from the same batch of money."

Frank looked excited. "If our theory's right, we're after the same bunch of thieves—not two separate gangs!"

"In that case," said Sam Radley, "it's a good thing we did get together on the mysteries."

The six friends continued their speculations until bedtime. The next morning after breakfast Frank and Joe decided to scout the Great Slave Lake area around Hay River. The Hardys flew off, turning east towards the mouth of Slave River.

As they flew along the southern shore, cruising at a low altitude, Joe said excitedly, "I see a group of men below. They're digging!"

"And it obviously isn't a well, from the rectangular shape of the hole," Frank commented, after circling over the figures below. "My guess is they're looking for something."

"If it's any kind of a legitimate enterprise, I imagine the Mounties at Hay River will know about it," Joe suggested. "Let's go back and check!"

When they returned and told their friends about the excavation, Sam Radley looked puzzled and at once called the Hay River RCMP station. When he returned, he said, "The officers there know nothing about any digging in this vicinity."

"Think the fellows you saw might be the thieves?" Tony asked Frank and Joe.

"We couldn't tell, of course," Frank replied. "How about our finding out, though?"

"I suggest we go up there tonight and investigate," Sam advised. "If the men are members of the gang, we don't want to scare them off."

The others concurred, and as soon as darkness had fallen that evening, the group set out. They went down to the dock and climbed into a boat with an outboard that Sam had hired. They used the engine until they drew near the spot where Frank and Joe had seen the diggers, then turned it off and rowed to shore. They beached the craft and crept along the sandy bank.

Suddenly Joe whispered, "Someone has a fire burning."

The group headed silently towards the glowing light. Like trained and skilful woodsmen, they approached without a sound. Ahead, six rough-looking, unshaven men were seated around a small, dying campfire. They evidently had just finished eating supper, and were leaning back, relaxed. The boys and Sam could not make out the men's features in the flickering, uncertain light.

Suddenly one of the campers spoke. "How's the translation of the stone coming?" he asked.

The man seated next to him shrugged and answered, "I'm making progress on the symbols, but slowly."

Frank turned to Sam Radley and whispered excitedly, "Symbols! These men must be the rune stone crooks!"

Radley nodded in agreement. "Okay, fellows," he murmured. "We may be able to take them off guard and capture the whole crew!"

In whispered agreement they decided that upon a signal from Radley, the pursuers would swoop down on their quarry. Chet nodded and rubbed his damp palms together, then set himself for the spring. But before Radley could say "charge," Chet's right toe caught on a vine and down he went with an "oomph" that resounded through the stillness of the dark forest.

"Oh, for Pete's sake!" Joe moaned.

"Get 'em!" Radley shouted.

The six strangers, however, had been amply warned, and were on their way before the boys could move in.

Snatching up their gear, they ran off into the darkness with muttered curses. Only one man straggled, and Joe pounced on him.

The rest clustered round Joe as he pulled the lone captive to his feet. The Hardys gasped and exclaimed in surprise, "*Kelly!*"

The thin, pale captive, not wearing a head bandage, showed no change of expression. He stared at the brothers with cold, blank eyes.

"What are you doing here?" Joe snapped. "Where's the Viking rune stone?"

Kelly remained sullenly silent.

"I guess he's not talking, boys," said Radley. "Let's search his duffle."

Joe picked up the canvas bag and pulled out the contents. Among the camping equipment he found an oddly-shaped package wrapped in brown paper. "Look!" he cried, untying it and holding up a slab of stone about eighteen inches long and six inches wide. It was covered with angular slanting lines.

"The rune stone!" Joe cried. "We've found it!"

Sam Radley and Tony, meanwhile, had securely bound the prisoner. They joined the others in scrutinizing the heavy stone and its strange markings.

"I guess one mystery is almost solved," Chet said, beaming.

"We'd better not count on that until we get Kelly back to Hay River and the stone's authenticity is verified," Sam Radley said.

The Hardys agreed. "Also," Frank said, "we have to track down the rest of the gang and find out whether or not they *are* the lodge thieves."

The captors took Kelly back to the boat with them, then motored swiftly to Hay River and went directly to the Mountie station with the fugitive from Bayport.

"Fine work, boys," the inspector on duty said, after hearing their story. "I'll hold this man and contact Police Chief Collig for verification."

The police took the still-silent prisoner into custody and said that they would let the Hardys and Radley know if he revealed anything under questioning.

When Frank and Joe showed them the stone, the Mounties were amazed and impressed by the find. "This *looks* like the real thing," the officer said, examining the carved tablet.

"I told you!" Chet exulted to his companions.

Sam Radley shook his head doubtfully. "I'm not convinced," he said.

"Nor am I," Frank declared. "Getting the stone back seemed too easy!"

"Well," Joe put in, "I'm not such a pessimist. I'm going to call Dad and tell him our news."

"Help yourself." The officer gestured to his telephone. Joe placed the call to his father in Edmonton.

"Good work!" said Mr Hardy, after hearing the full story. "But don't jump to conclusions!"

"All right, Dad," said Joe. "What's our next move?"

"You and Frank bring the stone to Edmonton," the detective replied. "Tell the others to stay in Hay River and keep out of sight. Ask Sam to contact me every day."

"Will do, Dad," Joe said. "See you soon. So long."

The Mountie agreed to let the boys take the stone along and had them sign a receipt for it.

After Joe had relayed his father's instructions to his companions, the whole group went to bed, tired from the excitement of the evening.

The next day the Hardys made the flight to Edmonton, arriving in the late afternoon. It was a smooth trip, and when they landed at the bustling airport, the boys hurried to the terminal. Frank carried the stone, carefully wrapped and tied.

As they rushed outside to a taxi, Frank stopped suddenly and pointed to a stack of newspapers on a stand close by. The Hardys stared in astonishment at a headline on the first page:

RUNE STONE FOUND
Hardy and Sons Return to States

· 12 ·

Offbeat Assignment

"COME on. Let's find out what this is all about!" Frank urged.

He and Joe took a taxi directly to the hotel where their father was staying. They walked swiftly through the foyer and took the lift to the detective's suite.

When Mr Hardy opened the door, both boys started to speak at once. "The rune stone case is solved?" Frank asked, and Joe said, "We saw the newspaper . . ."

They broke off in surprise when the detective smiled broadly. "Come in," he said. "I'll explain."

He shut the door. Frank and Joe quickly sat down. "The Edmonton newspaper," Mr Hardy continued, "has agreed to co-operate with us on this rune stone business. That headline about our returning home was to throw the thieves still at large off course." He chuckled. "In the same way it did you two."

"I get it," Frank said. "In case the stone is a fake."

Joe gave a low whistle. "Neat manoeuvre."

Frank then unwrapped the stone for his father's inspection. "When can we find out if this *is* genuine, Dad?"

"Perhaps tomorrow," the detective answered. "Mr Baker-Jones is much better, but the doctor in charge said that he should gain strength for a day before we talk to him."

Mr Hardy examined the stone and its markings closely.

"It certainly fits the description we got," Joe observed hopefully.

"Yes, it does," Mr Hardy agreed. "But we'll find out positively when Baker-Jones sees it."

That evening the three had dinner in the seclusion of the detective's hotel room. The next morning, as soon as the hospital would allow them to see the London Museum representative, the Hardys rushed over with the rune stone.

When they entered his room, Peter Baker-Jones was sitting up in bed. He looked pale and weak. The tall Englishman, who had a neatly clipped moustache, acknowledged Mr Hardy's introductions formally. But upon hearing why they had come, the patient's eyes brightened.

"The rune stone!" His voice shook with excitement. "Please! Let me see it quickly!"

Mr Hardy unwrapped the stone, and handed it to the expert on runic writings. The man put on his spectacles and carefully studied the tablet as the visitors waited tensely. A look of disappointment spread over the Englishman's face.

"This stone is not authentic," he said wearily, but with certainty. "I can tell by the sharp edges of the lines that it was not carved in the ninth century. It is a rather clever imitation."

"So—this Viking stone *was* faked—to decoy us off the case if the opportunity should arise," Joe said angrily. "Boy! Are they clever! We'll have to work fast before the crooks decipher the real one and find the treasure."

The Londoner was greatly agitated. "How can they be stopped?" he asked.

The Hardy's gave him a rapid account of their sleuthing, and the older detective said, "We'll let the gang think their ruse worked."

Frank now told the men of his belief that the lodge thieves operating round Great Slave Lake and the rune stone robbers were the same gang.

Mr Hardy smiled. "I agree. All we have to do is prove it—and capture the other gang members."

"How can we convince them we've given up the case," Joe asked, "if we continue to search for them?"

"The thieves must be made to believe we've returned to the States, and Mr Baker-Jones to England," the detective replied.

Mr Hardy then revealed a plan he had worked out. He suggested that the museum representative be taken secretly to a convalescent home outside Edmonton. "You can regain your strength there, Mr Baker-Jones, and when we find the real rune stone, we'll need your help for verification."

Mr Baker-Jones agreed to this suggestion. Fenton Hardy talked to the hospital authorities, and it was agreed that the Englishman would be moved quietly the next morning. When the Hardys left Baker-Jones, they told him that they would contact him at the convalescent home.

"Now let's get down to police headquarters," Mr Hardy said. "We're going to need one of their men."

When they arrived, the detective and his sons hurried to Inspector Knight's office. After an exchange of greetings and news, Mr Hardy asked him, "Is there a tall, thin man in your department we can borrow, Inspector?"

The man's eyebrows raised in surprise, but he answered, "Yes, there is. And you're welcome to use his services."

Frank grinned. "Dad, you're planning another impersonation—only not for yourself—right?"

"Exactly!" The detective went on to explain that he, Joe, and Frank would board a plane for the States, taking with them someone to pose as Peter Baker-Jones.

The inspector nodded understandingly. "And that's the role for my man. I'll get him now."

Knight left his office and returned with a tall policeman. "This is Officer Brent."

"Let's see how you look with a moustache," Mr Hardy said, after explaining the ruse. The detective handed Brent a false moustache.

When the officer held it in place, Joe burst out, "Terrific! With a hat and raincoat on, no one will know you're not Peter Baker-Jones!"

The group agreed to meet at the Hardys' hotel later that afternoon. They would take the plane bound for America, but would get off at Calgary.

The boys and Mr Hardy returned to their hotel. After a late lunch, they left for the airport with "Mr Baker-Jones," who was bundled up and walking slowly, the two boys supporting him. Joe carried a suitcase. When they boarded the plane, Mr Hardy whispered to

Frank, "I think our plan is working. I'm sure we're being watched!"

The airliner took off for the United States on schedule and when it dropped down at Calgary, the four alighted. The policeman went into the cloak-room, and when he rejoined the others, he was minus his disguise and carrying the suitcase. The Hardys said goodbye and thanked him as he rushed off to make the next flight back to Edmonton.

"We'll go straight to Hay River," Mr Hardy told his sons. "There's a flight by way of Saskatoon this afternoon."

They had dinner on the plane and arrived at Hay River late that night. It was still light, since the Arctic summer sun was just setting.

"We're notching up more miles than a veteran airline pilot," said Frank, yawning.

"We could use a good night's sleep," Mr Hardy agreed. "We'll hunt for Sam and the boys tomorrow."

The next morning the three sleuths were up early. At breakfast, Joe said, "The Mounties probably can tell us where Sam and the fellows are hiding."

"We'll check with them," his father said.

When they arrived at the RCMP station, the officer in charge told the famous detective and his sons the route to the hiding place of Radley and the three boys.

"They're in an abandoned schoolhouse on the northern outskirts of town," said the officer, spreading out a map on the desk. Pointing with a pencil, he continued, "If you follow this trail, you'll come to a field. The school house is right beyond that."

The Hardys thanked him and left the station, going

by way of back streets to the edge of town. They made their way through the high grass of the field and came upon a ramshackle wooden school building. When they knocked, there was no answer until Mr Hardy identified himself. Suddenly the door was pulled open and the trio stepped inside.

"Boy! Are we glad to see you back in one piece!" Chet grinned as they all shook hands.

"So far so good!" Joe laughed.

The Hardys' friends listened closely while the detectives related the recent events in Edmonton.

"I thought that stone was a fake," Sam said grimly.

"Have you found any clues to the gang's hide-out?" Joe asked him.

"Well, Chet might have," Radley replied.

It was the Hardys' turn to listen with keen interest as Chet told his story.

"Last night I sneaked out for food," the chubby boy said, "and went to the restaurant nearest here. I bought some food at the back entrance and on my way past the side of the place, I overheard some men talking by an open window in the dining room. One mentioned something about 'the stone.' "

Joe snapped his fingers. "Maybe the thieves hang out *there!*"

"I have an idea," Frank said. "Joe, you and I will apply for jobs in the restaurant's kitchen. If the thieves show up tonight, maybe we'll be able to capture them."

"I'll make a great odd-job boy." Joe grinned. "Frank, you can be dishwasher!"

"Thanks a lot!" Frank grimaced. "But anything in the line of duty! All right, let's apply!"

The two boys left, but returned to the schoolhouse an hour later with news that they had received part-time jobs and would start work that night.

"The restaurant isn't open until evening," Joe explained.

At the appointed time the brothers reported and got busy with their chores. At every opportunity they observed the patrons in the small dining room. To their disappointment neither boy saw nor heard anything suspicious.

It was near midnight when Joe, mopping the floor by the half-open kitchen door, noticed two men come into the dining room. As they walked over to join several hard-looking men seated at a table, Joe heard one of the pair ask, "What'll become of Kelly? Do you know?"

Joe beckoned to his brother. Frank hurried over. The boys pressed against the wall near the door, straining to catch every word that was said.

"Kelly's biding his time," the second man was saying. "We'll meet him at the place now that the Hardys have gone back!"

Was it possible these men did not know Kelly was in jail?

"What place?" someone asked. The boys recognized the voice of the man who had spoken first.

There was no answer, but the boys heard the ring of a coin hitting the tabletop. Joe cautiously peered round the corner.

Bang! A waiter balancing a tray loaded with dishes hit the door from the other side. The tray crashed to the floor.

The waiter, furious, pushed the door wide open to reveal the Hardy boy crouching in the entrance. Joe, taken by surprise, saw that the group of tough-looking men in the dining room were staring at him.

Suddenly one jumped up. "It's one of those Hardy kids!" he yelled. "Get him!"

· 13 ·

Explosion!

"LET's go!" Frank dashed for the back door. Joe dropped the mop and ran after him.

As their pursuers leaped towards the kitchen, the waiter turned to retrieve the tray, and collided with the first man. The two went down with a thud, landing on the floor among the broken dishes.

"Blast!" cried a burly fellow behind them, and pushed past the two into the kitchen.

The Hardys heard the commotion as they hurried outside and into a dark alleyway behind the building.

"This way," Frank whispered, as he whirled to the left. Joe followed.

They ran round to the front and across the road, passing through the light streaming from the window of the restaurant. Suddenly they heard the door bang open and a harsh voice yell, "There they go!"

"After them!" came a raucous cry.

The boys jumped into a deep ditch on the other side of the road. As they darted along the narrow gully they could hear pounding footsteps behind them. A short distance ahead Frank saw a culvert just large enough for them to crawl into.

"In here," he said, and jumped into the opening.

Joe leaped in after him, and the brothers crouched in the dark, damp space. They held their breath until all the pursuers had run past and continued on. In a few moments the sound of footsteps died away and the men's voices faded into the distance.

"Let's go!" Joe urged.

"Wait!" cautioned his brother. "More of the gang may be coming. We'll crawl through and out the other end."

The boys had just pulled themselves out of the culvert when they heard a yell from the spot where they had been hiding.

"Here's a culvert!" came a man's excited voice. "Search it!"

Then another voice came from the darkness. "You look there and I'll check down the road."

Tensely the boys waited for the man's approach. "We'll jump him," Frank muttered.

A few seconds later they heard footsteps. Ready for the attack, the boys waited until the man was almost upon them, then leaped out.

Frank clamped a hand over the man's mouth and Joe made a flying tackle round his knees, bringing him to the ground. The Hardys pinioned his arms tightly.

Joe whipped out his handkerchief and gagged the husky captive. Then the boys hauled him to his feet.

"Let's get him to the Mounties," Joe urged.

"Right," Frank agreed.

The boys marched the prisoner through the deserted back streets to the RCMP station. When they entered the station, the officer at the desk looked up in surprise.

"We're sure this man is one of the rune stone thieves," Frank told him. "There were some other men after us. Sorry we couldn't capture them."

The desk officer hurried to call the inspector, who came over to the office immediately. He searched the prisoner carefully and pulled out a wallet.

"Hank Fogert! Is that your name?" the inspector asked the surly-looking man. There was no answer.

"He's a United States citizen, boys," the inspector said, "according to these papers!"

Frank was sure the man was one of those whom the Hardys had surprised at the campsite. He might know about the mysterious digging operations. Frank faced the prisoner and asked, "What were you and your pals digging for on the lake shore?"

Fogert looked startled, but would say nothing.

"Well, Fogert, we'll give you time in a cell," the officer said brusquely. "Then maybe you'll feel like talking. The charges against you are attempted assault and battery and suspicion of larceny."

The prisoner glared defiantly as he shuffled off with a guard. At the door he looked round at the Hardys. "Kelly will get even with you!" he snarled, then was led away.

"Kelly must be a pretty important guy in that gang," Frank remarked. "Maybe he's the top man."

"He must be at least one of the lieutenants," Joe surmised, as the brothers walked down the front steps of the police station.

They returned to the schoolhouse to find everyone wide awake waiting for them.

"Did anything happen at the restaurant?" Chet asked eagerly.

"Oh, nothing much," Frank said, grinning at his brother.

"No, nothing much," Joe said. "We just captured another one of the rune stone thieves!"

After excited exclamations from Mr Hardy and their friends, Frank and Joe told about the chase and capture of Hank Fogert. When they had finished their account, Sam said, "Great work! We're really whittling down that gang!"

"Yes, but we still haven't found the real stone," Frank remarked. "I vote that first thing in the morning we investigate the shore where the crooks were digging."

It was decided to separate into two groups. Sam, with Frank, Biff and Tony, would go to the digging site to learn, if possible, what the gang was up to. The others would remain at the schoolhouse hideout.

The seven crawled into their sleeping bags. They awoke at sunrise, and after eating a hearty breakfast, Sam and the three boys set out. They hurried to the cove where Sam had secreted his boat and climbed in.

The craft hugged the shore of Great Slave Lake, and presently Frank pointed ahead. "There's where we spotted the diggers."

In a few minutes the boat was beached. The foursome found the rectangular excavation and examined it closely.

"What do you suppose those guys were hunting for?" Tony asked.

"The Viking treasure mentioned on the rune stone!" Frank frowned. "That is, if they've deciphered the symbols."

"I wonder what the treasure is?" Biff mused.

"Let's search in the hole," Frank said, jumping down. "Maybe there's a clue here!"

The others joined him and spread out along the narrow excavation.

Suddenly Tony called out, "Here's something!" He bent down. "It's a wire!"

Frank was standing near him. As Tony grabbed the wire and pulled, Frank yelled, "Look out!" and leaping aside, pulled Tony to the ground with him.

Bah-room! A huge cloud of dust and pebbles rose high into the air and the earth shuddered with an underground explosion. Frank and Tony, though shaken, were unhurt. As the dust cleared, they saw Sam and Biff some distance away, struggling to their feet.

"Wh-a-at happened?" Biff demanded, when he and Sam ran up.

"A booby trap!" Frank stated grimly, rising. "We're lucky to be alive!"

Tony got to his feet, brushing the dust from his clothes. "What caused the explosion?" he asked.

"Dynamite!" Sam replied tensely. "They're really eager to get rid of us, so they came back and booby-trapped this spot, knowing we'd investigate it."

"That wire I pulled triggered off the blast!" Tony realized in horror. "Thanks to me, we could have been blown sky-high!"

Just then Frank's attention was attracted by a

tattered piece of paper sticking out of the dirt. He picked it up.

"A map!" said Frank, as the others gathered round to look. "It covers this whole area."

"There's Hay River," Tony observed. "And there's Fort Smith and the Wood Buffalo National Park."

"Probably dropped by the thieves," Sam surmised. "But nothing special is marked on it."

"Wood Buffalo Park," Frank repeated thoughtfully. "Of course! Wood Buffalo Park!"

"What do you mean?" Biff asked.

"When Joe and I were working in the restaurant, one of the gang asked where 'the place' was. The answer was the sound of a coin hitting the table."

"So?" Tony looked mystified.

"Well, I've had a hunch it was a signal or code, and I've been trying to figure out exactly what kind. I think I have it." Frank continued, "It could have been a nickel—an American *buffalo* nickel!"

"Bet you're right!" Tony cried out excitedly. "The gang is hiding out in Wood Buffalo Park!"

"With the stolen rune stone!" Biff added.

Back at the schoolhouse, the four related their morning's experience. Chet turned pale. "Dynamite!" he quavered. "Those guys must be getting desperate."

Mr Hardy said gravely, "We must round up the rest of them—and soon."

Frank now told his theory about Buffalo National Park.

"Sounds logical," said Mr Hardy. "I believe it's worth checking out!"

"How?" Joe asked.

"Maybe we can trick Fogert into divulging some information," his father replied.

The detective and his sons went immediately to the RCMP station. When they arrived, the officer in charge agreed to let them question the prisoner.

"We got no response from him," he said grimly. "Maybe you'll have better luck. I'll bring him in."

As Hank Fogert was led in by the officer and a police guard, Frank greeted him casually. "The boss sends his best from Wood Buffalo Park," he said.

Fogert stopped suddenly, obviously startled by the remark. "How—" he began, looking puzzled. Suddenly the expression on his face turned from one of surprise to fierce anger when he realized that he had been trapped.

"Why, you—" he snarled, and lunged towards Frank.

·14·

Buffalo Park Clue

"No, you don't!" Mr Hardy stepped quickly in front of the thug.

The detective fell back, however, as the burly prisoner threw his full weight against him. Mr Hardy instantly regained his balance, but by this time the police guard had overpowered Fogert. Nevertheless, he kicked out viciously and struck the detective on his kneecap.

"Take Fogert to his cell!" Mr Hardy said. "He has already told us what we wanted to know."

Fogert jerked his head like a snake ready to strike, and staring at the Hardys with hatred gleaming in his eyes, he said sneeringly, "We're not through yet—not by a long shot." The guard led him off.

Joe turned to the inspector and asked, "Is anyone in the cell next to Fogert?"

"Just a petty thief. I doubt if he knows anything about Fogert, but you're welcome to question him."

"Thanks," Mr Hardy said. "We will."

The detective and his sons followed the officer down a corridor to a small, dimly lighted room fronted by long steel bars. A wizened little man sat forlornly on a narrow bed. He looked up glumly when the detective addressed him. "Has the prisoner next door talked to you?"

"Nope," the man answered. "The only time that Yank talks is in his sleep. Snores and talks all night long," the man complained. "I haven't had any shut-eye since he came."

"Thank you," Mr Hardy said, turning abruptly and walking back down the hall. His sons followed quickly.

"What's up?" Joe asked when they were back in the Mounties' office.

"I think we're going to listen in on Hank Fogert tonight," Mr Hardy replied. "He might say something interesting in his sleep."

"Terrific idea, Dad!" Frank said enthusiastically.

The Hardys conferred with the Mountie inspector about the idea. The officer agreed, and it was decided to have tape-recording equipment and a microphone hidden in Fogert's cell.

"Let's hope the noisy 'Yank' tells us more in his sleep than he does when he's awake," Joe said as they started back to the schoolhouse.

"And that what he says will give us a solid clue," Frank added, "either about the Viking stone or where the rest of the gang are."

The Hardys' friends were enthusiastic when they heard of the hidden-recorder setup and discussed this new angle in the case. After lunch Mr Hardy looked round the group. With a chuckle he said:

"I think we deserve a little holiday from detective work. How about trying some of the famous fishing in this area?"

Everyone cheered the suggestion, and spent the

afternoon on the waters of Great Slave Lake. When the fishermen returned to the schoolhouse, Chet and Biff carried creels full of lake trout and grayling.

"*This* is the life," Chet declared later, as he and the others ate a hearty supper of succulent fried fish.

"Enjoy it now." Joe grinned. "Something tells me we won't have much chance to fish from now on."

Chet groaned in mock dismay. "Meaning—back to the mystery full time."

"Tomorrow bright and early," Frank assured him.

Immediately after breakfast the next morning, Mr Hardy, Joe and Frank hurried directly to the RCMP station. The officer greeted them and indicated a tape recorder on his desk. "All set for you to play back," he said. "I cut out most of the silent parts."

Frank started the machine, and the four bent over the tape, listening intently. There was a short interval of quiet—then a raspy muttering could be heard.

"Fogert!" Joe hissed excitedly.

Another silence, followed by some unintelligible phrases. The Hardys glanced at one another in disappointment—was their plan to prove a fruitless one?

Suddenly they tensed as Fogert's recorded voice spoke again. "Stone—shay," he mumbled. "—Dulac— lake—"

The listeners strained their ears, but no further words could be distinguished from the rest of the tape. The recorder was shut off and Joe burst out, "Stone! Dulac! *Abner* Dulac? The *rune* stone?"

Elatedly the Hardys speculated on the words muttered by the sleeping prisoner.

"I think Dulac is the key word," Frank stated. "He

and Fogert know each other! Which means—Dulac is one of the rune stone gang."

Joe agreed. "And trailed us from Edmonton after Caribou spotted him."

Quickly they revealed what they knew of the unscrupulous trapper.

"Shay—lake—" Frank repeated. "I don't get 'shay' —and *which* lake? I doubt the gang would dare go back to Great Slave—" He broke off as a sudden thought struck him. "Say! Maybe the lake's in Wood Buffalo Park!"

Mr Hardy concurred. "I suggest heading straight for the park."

"You bet, Dad!" Joe said eagerly.

"Shall we go back to Fort Smith and pick up the float plane for the trip?" Frank asked.

"Yes," his father replied. "Flying is the best way. We can check with the Mounties there, and get a permit to enter the park."

The Hardys hastened to the schoolhouse and briefed their friends on the latest findings. The group had a quick lunch, packed their rucksacks, and went to the Hay River airport. They were in time to board the early-afternoon plane for Fort Smith.

When they landed at Fort Smith, Frank went to the terminal and telephoned Corporal Fergus.

"The lodge gang seems to be operating near the Yellowknife area," the Mountie reported. "Two lodges there have been robbed, but the thieves have eluded us."

"Yellowknife?" Joe repeated in surprise, when his brother relayed Corporal Fergus's message. "That's way up on the other side of Great Slave Lake—the gang is back in that area! Why?"

"You think we've been wrong about there being just *one* gang?" Sam asked.

Mr Hardy frowned. "Perhaps. But it could also be a manoeuvre on their part to split our forces."

"I see what you mean, sir," Chet put in. "Now we don't know whether to go to Yellowknife or to Wood Buffalo Park."

"Exactly. Well, we can't take any chances," Mr Hardy said. "Sam—you, Biff and Tony go on up to Yellowknife and check on the gang's activities there. Chet, Frank, and Joe—you scout Wood Buffalo Park."

"What are you going to do, Dad?" Joe asked.

"I'm going to stay here in Fort Smith," the detective answered. "I'll maintain radio contact with both groups. Frank, you can hire a short-wave portable at the Hudson's Bay store. Sam, of course, has his own. I'd join you on the trip into the park, but I must admit my knee's been giving me a few twinges since my bout with Fogert. I wouldn't be good for any long hikes!"

"You take it easy, Dad," Joe advised. "We're going to nab those thieves one place or another!"

"We'd better get moving," Frank said.

"Right," Mr Hardy agreed. "Sam, there's a flight to Yellowknife leaving in half an hour. You three can take it."

The two groups separated, with Biff, Tony and Sam going off to buy tickets for the trip to Yellowknife.

"We'll be in touch with you soon, sir," Biff said to Mr Hardy as they all exchanged farewells.

Then Frank, Joe and Chet, accompanied by Mr

Hardy, headed for the Wood Buffalo Park office. When they arrived, a helicopter was just landing in the small clearing outside the administration office. A stocky, muscular man, with a ruddy, weathered face, stepped from the cockpit. He smiled at the Hardys and Chet as he jumped to the ground.

"Hello," he said, coming towards them. "I'm Breen Connor. Were you looking for me?"

Mr Hardy introduced himself and the boys and shook hands with the rugged-looking park superintendent.

"Have you had any recent visitors applying for passes into the park?" Frank asked the official.

"Yes, Frank," Mr Connor answered. "Quite a few. Only one stranger though, a fellow named Fontain."

When Breen Connor described the man, the brothers and Chet looked excited. "That sounds like Abner Dulac!" Joe cried. "Where was he going?"

"To Shag Lake," Breen Connor replied. "He seemed to know the country well."

"Shay—Shag! *That's* what Fogert mumbled in his sleep!" Frank exclaimed. "Joe, we have a terrific clue!"

·15·

The Grey Terror

"SHAG Lake!" Chet echoed in excitement. "That must be the gang's hideout!"

"The sooner we get there the better!" Frank said eagerly.

"How about today?" Joe turned to the park superintendent. "Can you issue us a pass now?"

"Yes," replied Breen Connor. "But if you're going up there, you'd better study the area first. It's wild, dangerous country!"

He took the visitors into his office, and from a desk drawer pulled out a sheaf of papers. After he gave the required permit to the boys, the visitors sat down round a large table. The official brought over a detailed map of the area and spread it out.

"Shag Lake is named after the shaggy buffalo in this area," Breen Connor told them, pointing to the lake, in the park's southeastern corner. "Watch those buffalo," he warned. "They're ferocious and so are the wolves."

"Great!" Chet muttered, growing a shade paler.

"The Shag Lake region is strewn with great boulders, a result of an Ice Age moraine."

"It sounds like a good place for a hideout," Joe said.

Breen Connor nodded in agreement, then asked, "How do you plan to get into the park?"

"We're going by float plane," Frank answered. "Where is the best place to keep it?"

"Here on the south shore," the man said, pointing, "is a small cove. It's barely visible from the air. You could taxi in there and tie the plane to the rocks."

"Fine," Frank said, standing up. "Thanks for all the information, sir. It'll be a big help."

Mr Hardy and his sons started to leave. As they walked outside, Breen Connor called after them.

"Be careful, boys!" he advised. "The buffalo are often uneasy at this time of year. If you don't bother them, they shouldn't bother you, but anything unusual might start a stampede. Good luck!"

"We'll need it!" Joe remarked, as the group hurried over to the Hudson's Bay store. Here they bought provisions, hired a short-wave radio, and as a precaution, several rifles. Next Joe phoned the airport. The float plane would be fuelled and ready for them in half an hour.

After eating dinner, the detective went with the boys to the airport jetty. "Keep me informed via radio," he reminded the three boys, as they climbed aboard. "And be careful!"

"Sure thing, Dad. So long!"

With Joe at the controls, they took off and headed straight for Wood Buffalo Park. It was just dusk when they flew over it in the direction of Shag Lake. Joe located the hidden cove on the first pass. As he turned for his final approach, he switched off the engine.

"I'm going to make a dead-stick landing," he told

Frank and Chet, "so that if the gang is down there they won't hear us."

With nothing but the whistle of the wind in the wings to betray its presence, the float plane swooped down over the trees. Joe pulled back on the stick as the plane dropped into the water for a perfect landing.

"Well done, Joe," Frank said. The aircraft was pointed towards shore and drifted into its berth in the cove neatly and silently.

Quickly the boys unloaded their gear and moved far into the woods, away from the plane. Frank and Joe walked ahead, while Chet covered their trail with leaves and brush as they went along. When they reached a small clearing located near some protective rocks, the boys set up camp.

"Let's take turns standing watch," Frank said, as they spread out their sleeping bags.

"I'll take first watch," Chet offered. He sat down and leaned against a nearby tree.

Frank and Joe were soon asleep and the camp was quiet. "It's almost too quiet," Chet told himself uneasily.

But as the time passed uneventfully, and the bright, arctic moon rose, the chubby boy relaxed. Suddenly he sat upright. "What's that?" Chet's hair stood on end as an eerie howling came to his ears.

The bloodcurdling sound again floated in the still night. Chet sat rigid, as the howling came closer and closer. "I'd better wake up the fellows," he decided. But before he had a chance to do so, Chet saw a stealthy movement in the shadows near the Hardys. He gulped, standing up slowly and peering into the darkness.

Suddenly Chet saw two red glowing eyes staring at him. The next moment a hulking, grey shape emerged into the moonlight and sniffed around. A chill of terror went down Chet's spine as he realized the danger he was facing.

"A wolf!"

Quickly he nestled the rifle stock against his cheek and centred the animal in his gunsights. The grey beast stood still, his jaws open and his head down, ready to attack.

Chet increased the pressure on the trigger, squinting his eyes and taking careful aim. Then he released his grip abruptly. A rifleshot would surely kill the wolf, but it would also warn the thieves that the boys were in the vicinity.

Leaning over, Chet picked up a large rock. With careful aim, he hurled it at the animal. The missile hit the wolf squarely on the side of the head. Giving a sharp yelp of pain, he sped away.

"What was that?" Frank called out, as he and Joe awoke with a start. They scrambled from their bags and jumped up.

"A wolf," Chet explained, somewhat shakily. "I didn't want to risk a shot in case anyone heard, so I threw a rock at him."

"Smart thinking, pal," Joe praised him, and Frank added, "Took a lot of nerve, too. You deserve a medal, Chet."

Their friend beamed. "But I think I need some sleep, fellows," he said. "You keep away the next wolf!"

A quick search of the area proved that the creature

was not lurking nearby, and the boys settled down again, with first Frank, then Joe on watch.

"I'll never manage to get to sleep tonight after all the excitement," Chet proclaimed.

Frank and Joe winked to each other. They knew that nothing could stop Chet from getting to sleep—not even a wolf attack.

As soon as it was daylight the three friends began their search for the gang's hideout. They picked their way along silently, being careful to stay under cover. Just as the boys started along the base of a hill, Frank, who was leading, waved for the others to stop.

"Behind that boulder, quick!" he hissed. "Someone's coming."

As the boys dropped behind the huge rock, they heard heavy footsteps approaching, then rough voices. The Hardys, crouching, peered cautiously round the boulder. Four men were trudging in single file past their hiding place. Two were burly and husky, another pudgy and grizzled-looking. As the fourth man came into view, Joe started.

"That's Dulac!" he whispered to Frank. "The others look like the men we saw in the restaurant."

All four men were carrying rifles as they tramped on towards the woods. As soon as they were out of sight among the trees, the three boys crept quietly from cover, and turned to track the men.

"Listen!" Chet stopped suddenly.

They heard a faint cry. "Pretty far away," Joe said.

"More wolves?" Chet looked apprehensive.

"I don't think that's any wolf!" Frank said seriously. "Sounds like a human voice! It's a cry for help!"

·16·

Secret Ingredient

"A CRY for help!" Chet echoed, his eyes widening. "Who could it be?"

"There's one way to find out," Frank said. "Let's go!" He headed in the direction of the voice, which called out again at just that moment. Moving quickly, he, Joe and Chet followed the trail Dulac and his friends had been travelling.

Once again they heard the cry, though fainter this time. "Hurry!" Joe urged. "Someone must be hurt!"

The three spread out, covering the woods circling the narrow, winding trail. Suddenly Joe shouted:

"Over here! It's Caribou!"

Frank and Chet ran over. Shocked, they saw that the husky trapper lay beneath a spruce tree, bound hand and foot with rawhide thongs. His eyes were closed and his head moved from side to side. He groaned as if in pain.

"He has a bad gash on his forehead," Frank said, bending down to untie their friend. "He's semi-conscious."

"Those rats must have left him here for the wolves," Chet said hotly, as he pulled out his canteen to bathe Caribou's head.

"We could take better care of him at the plane," Joe said. "Let's carry him there."

The Hardys and Chet lifted the heavy man and slowly made their way back to the float plane. The boys' muscles ached with the burden of both their equipment and the unconscious woodsman. But finally they reached the secret cove. After they laid the trapper down in the shade of a tree, Chet got out the first-aid kit and cleaned and bandaged Caribou's wound. After a few minutes the French-Canadian stirred and blinked his eyes. He tried to sit up, but sank back with a moan.

"Easy," Joe cautioned him.

"*Bon tonnerre!*" Caribou exclaimed weakly. "My head is split!" Then he looked at the boys. "My friends! How did you get here?"

The three grinned at him reassuringly. "We'll tell you later," Frank said. "Lucky thing we heard you calling. What happened?"

"I trail Dulac to park," the trapper replied. "Early this morning, follow him again, then suddenly four men jump out from the bush behind me and hit me on the head. That is the last thing I remember." His face grew flushed. "I was a fool!" he stormed. "Dulac and Kelly must be the masked men who took the stone and money."

"Who are the men with Dulac now?" Frank asked.

"All thieves—they have the rune stone!" Caribou answered. "Last night I sneak up on their hideout—a cave. I stood outside and hear them talk about the stone."

Caribou rubbed his head gingerly. "Other three men called Mike, Red, and Fats."

"Must be the guys we saw with Dulac a short while ago," Joe said excitedly. "But they didn't have the stone."

"No," Caribou said, "because it is in their cave. I hear them complain they cannot read the message on it. Kelly was to translate it but he got caught."

"Did you hear anything else?" Chet put in.

"*Oui*," Caron replied gravely. "They will kidnap Monsieur Baker-Jones. Make him tell what the stone says."

"What!" Joe exclaimed. "I thought we had the gang fooled about Baker-Jones!"

Caribou looked doubtful. "The robbers think he is in Edmonton."

"What'll we do now?" Chet asked the Hardys.

"Get the rune stone," Frank replied coolly. "How do you feel, Caribou?"

"It takes more than a bump on the head to keep Caribou away," the trapper said, rising to his feet. "We go to the robbers' cave!"

The three boys eagerly fell into step behind him. Swiftly and silently they followed the trapper for what seemed like miles. The trail led round the shore of Shag Lake, and north into the woods. Caribou strode to the foot of a hill, stopped, and pointed.

"The cave is over this hill," he whispered. "If I can fool the crooks, you boys run inside and try to find the stone. I will meet you at your plane."

"Right," Frank said. "We're ready."

Caribou climbed the slope and went round some huge boulders to approach the hideout from the opposite direction. The boys, meanwhile, crawled straight up to the top of the hill where they could see the mouth of the cave. By this time Caribou had edged close to the entrance. He stood up and hurled a stone into the hideout.

A moment later Dulac emerged. He stared out into the sunlight, his hand shading his eyes from the glare.

"Dulac!" Caribou roared. "You goat! You weasel!" Then the big trapper staggered back, pretending to be overcome by weakness.

"It's Caron!" Dulac shouted back into the cave. "He's free!" Dulac ran towards the trapper, who began to back away from the cave. Three men emerged from the hideout and took up the chase.

Soon Caribou and his pursuers were out of sight behind the boulders. Frank, Joe and Chet sped to the cave and dashed inside.

"Hurry!" Frank said breathlessly. "We haven't much time. We must find the rune stone!"

The three boys searched frantically through the knapsacks lying on the rocky floor.

"Hey! The book stolen from the Bayport Library." Joe held up a red volume he had pulled from a canvas sack. "*Rune Stones and Viking Symbols* by Peter Baker-Jones!"

"Keep it, Joe," Frank said. "We're on the right track."

He began shaking out four bedrolls, while Chet rooted through boxes of gear. When they were through, Frank shook his head disgustedly. "No luck! The stone isn't here!" he said.

Just then Chet spotted a long loaf of crusty bread on top of a box. "I'm starving!" he muttered.

"Chet! We must get out of here!" Frank warned, as his chubby friend hacked at the loaf with a knife. *Scrape!*

"Talk about stale bread!" Chet exclaimed, attacking the loaf again. "Hard as a rock!"

"Rock!" Frank echoed, grabbing the loaf. To his amazement, the whole top came off in his hand. Nestled inside was a long, odd-shaped stone with angular markings.

"The rune stone!" Frank cried out.

"This must be the real one!" Joe said joyfully. "Chet, it's a good thing you became hungry!"

Frank scooped up the rune stone, and clutching it tightly, led the way as they all fled from the cave. As they headed for the hilltop, the boys saw two of the gang coming up the other side of the slope.

"Whew!" Chet panted. "We got out of there just in time!"

He and the Hardys sprinted silently through the high grass and into the woods. They followed the lightly blazed trail that led to the secret cove.

"Oh, no!" Joe suddenly exclaimed, stopping in his tracks. "I've dropped the book!"

"There's no time to go back, Joe," Frank said, urging him forward.

The boys continued along the path and finally reached the hidden float plane. Frank jumped into the cockpit. As Joe and Chet were climbing up, Caribou came crashing through the bushes at the edge of the cove.

"*Bon tonnerre, mes amis!*" the trapper shouted. "Hurry! There is no time to spare!"

He rushed to the plane and gave it a mighty push, then jumped in. The craft floated out into the cove.

"Go, Frank!" screamed the French-Canadian, his beard jutting out with excitement. "Dulac off the track now, but not for long."

Frank hit the starter and the engine caught at once. Not worrying about the wind, Frank pressed home the throttle. He would have to make a crosswind take-off.

The roar of the plane was loud in their ears as they saw Dulac and his men appear on the shore. The boys watched Dulac raise his rifle. They could not hear the shots but they saw the wind snatch a wisp of smoke away from the muzzle.

Suddenly Frank felt the aircraft dip slightly to starboard. He knew they were not up on the step and the shock had not been hard enough for them to have hit a piece of floating debris.

"It's the floats!" Joe shouted. "He's hit the floats! If they flood, we'll never get off the water!"

·17·

Viking Message

"THE floats!" Frank thought. He knew they would be divided into compartments. But how well would the bulkheads between each compartment hold if more than one was flooded?

The young pilot felt the extra weight of water on the right side of the aircraft dragging it to starboard. He knew he was in trouble.

Placing enough pressure on the rudder bar to straighten out the plane, Frank gently forced the stick over to the left. The engine was labouring against the extra weight, but the plane was picking up speed through the water.

He felt the right wing lift. As it did so, the starboard float cleared the water and the left float came up on the step.

Immediately the plane picked up speed, and as Frank eased the stick back a hair, they were airborne and away.

Frank pushed the stick forward to drop the nose and pick up more speed. Then he pulled back and they were swooping over the trees.

"Whew!" Chet breathed a sigh of relief. "Now, what about the landing at Fort Smith?"

"Shouldn't be any trouble," Frank said. "Any water that got in has probably run out by now."

Joe radioed a message to his father that they were on the way and would meet him at the RCMP station. After setting down at Fort Smith, the boys and Caribou went directly to headquarters.

Mr Hardy and Corporal Fergus were waiting for them. Quickly Frank gave the details of the gang's attack on Caribou and their narrow escape in the plane.

"And," Joe said, grinning, "we brought you a present, Dad! Right, Frank?"

"You bet." Frank had rolled his sweater round the rune stone. Now he unwrapped the ancient tablet and handed it to his father.

"Great work, boys!" said the detective in delighted surprise. "I can hardly believe it!"

"Congratulations!" added Corporal Fergus.

"We're pretty sure this stone is genuine," Frank told the men, "since the thieves went to the trouble of hiding it in a loaf of bread." He grinned. "Chet had to go without something to eat."

The plump boy feigned a look of starvation. "At this point I *could* eat rocks."

Mr Hardy suggested that he and the boys have a quick bite at a nearby restaurant. After eating, Frank said, "Dad, let's take this stone to Mr Baker-Jones as soon as possible, and also warn him to be on his guard against the thieves' kidnapping plan. Maybe we should notify the police."

"I'll do that," said Mr Hardy, "and we should be on our way. There's a flight out of here early this evening. Will you call, Joe, and make reservations for four?"

"Sure thing, Dad."

"Please, Mr Hardy," Caribou spoke up. "I go with you to Edmonton. Dulac and his gang will not give up the stone so easy. You will be in danger. I will protect you!"

"We appreciate your offer, Caribou," Mr Hardy said. "But with your long whiskers I'm afraid the crooks would spot us a mile off!"

Caribou grinned. "I can get a shave and haircut right away." He looked at the detective hopefully.

"Fine." Mr Hardy smiled. "Joe, make that reservation for five."

The trapper beamed and strode off. When he returned in half an hour, he had short hair and was clean shaven.

"Caribou," Joe said in amazement, "I'd hardly recognize you myself!"

The French-Canadian grinned. "I am something like a plucked chicken, no?" he asked.

They all laughed, then left to get ready for the trip. The boys returned the hired equipment to Bill Stone and took fresh clothes from their suitcases at the Hudson's Bay Company store. Later, they met Mr Hardy at his hotel.

"Any word from Sam and the fellows?" Joe asked his father.

The detective said Radley had just reported by radio that an unidentified float plane had been sighted. "Sam thinks the rest of the gang might be using it," Mr Hardy added. "He and the boys are working on that angle."

The flight to Edmonton was nonstop, but it was too late for the group to visit Peter Baker-Jones in the convalescent home that night.

Directly after breakfast the following morning, the five left for the suburbs of Edmonton. When they arrived at the large, old house that was now converted to a nursing home, they inquired at the reception desk and the attendant said that they might go right up to see the rune stone expert. Caribou waited downstairs to keep watch for anyone suspicious.

"We won't mention the kidnap threat to Mr Baker-Jones," Mr Hardy decided. When he and the boys entered the patient's room, they found him sitting up in an easy chair, reading.

"Good morning," said the Englishman, nodding formally at the visitors. He looked much stronger and had more colour than when they had last seen him.

"I have a surprise for you." Frank smiled and brought out the tablet. "We hope you'll find this to be the genuine rune stone."

Mr Baker-Jones's reserve gave way to great enthusiasm. He listened with keen interest to the boys' account of their adventures in finding the relic in the cave hideout.

"My word!" he exclaimed. "You have taken great risks in this case. If only those scoundrels can be brought to justice!"

"We'll see to that!" Joe declared tersely.

The patient arose, took the stone, and placed it carefully on the table. He scrutinized the odd markings, as the Hardys and Chet waited with bated breath for his verdict.

"Hmm." Mr Baker-Jones ran his fingers across the characters cut into the surface of the stone, then lifted it as if trying to determine the weight. He looked very carefully once more at the markings. Then, finally, very deliberately, the museum representative placed the tablet on the table and removed his glasses.

"Well?" said Joe, unable to suppress his curiosity any longer. "*Is* it real?"

"Unquestionably genuine," the expert pronounced. "Authentic ninth-century runic tablet."

"Wahoo!" Joe cheered.

"Terrific!" cried Chet.

"We've solved half the mystery, at least," Frank put in elatedly.

Mr Hardy smiled, obviously pleased at his sons' and Chet's discovery, then turned to Mr Baker-Jones and asked him, "Can you translate the Viking symbols?"

"I believe so," the runic expert replied. He put on his glasses and bent over the tablet. After some minutes of intent study, he straightened. "Roughly, the symbols say a ship is hidden in a cove near a river which meets a knife-shaped body of water, on the north shore of a great lake. Apparently the vessel, which contained treasure, was sunk!"

"That ship must be what the crooks were digging for, but without this translation they couldn't find the right place," Joe said.

"If they had studied my book more thoroughly," said Mr Baker-Jones, "they might have found the answer."

"Of course Kelly, *their* translator," Joe said, "is in jail."

Frank, meanwhile, had been pondering the message on the ancient Viking tablet. "A great lake," he murmured. "Would that be Great Slave Lake, do you think?"

"Well now, let's think. The northwestern part of Great Slave Lake *is* shaped like a knife blade," Joe said.

"And the cove must be near Yellowknife," Frank added. "That's where a river runs into the lake."

Suddenly the group in the room were startled by loud voices coming from downstairs. *Crash!*

The Hardys dashed into the hall and down the stairs two at a time. They found Caribou and a man struggling on the floor. The huge trapper was furious.

"*Bon tonnerre!*" he shouted as he tussled with his wiry opponent.

"Caribou!" Mr Hardy exclaimed. "What happened?" Together, the boys broke the giant's grip on the other man, whom they pulled to his feet.

"Abner Dulac!" Joe exclaimed in amazement.

The captive wore a dark suit, and on the floor lay a physician's black bag.

"That's Dulac, all right!" Caribou snorted in disgust. He stepped towards his adversary and kicked the black bag open. A pistol tumbled out. The trapper glowered at his old enemy.

"He sneak in here to steal the rune stone, I bet! He always was no good."

"Good work, Caribou!" Joe said. 'I'll call the police."

When several officers arrived and handcuffed Dulac, he sneered at his captors.

"You think you have beaten us! But you haven't. Kelly has escaped!" he gloated. "We smuggled a small gun to him in his food. We'll get the Viking treasure first!"

·18·

Whistler's Signal

"KELLY *has escaped!*" Frank repeated in astonishment as Dulac was led off. "Think that's true Dad?"

Mr Hardy frowned. "I'll call the Hay River police right away and find out." He hurried to the reception office to use the telephone.

In a few minutes the detective rejoined the boys. "Dulac was right," he said. "Kelly escaped from the Hay River jail two nights ago by overpowering a guard."

"What if he deciphered the symbols before we found the stone?" Frank asked worriedly.

"Or, he could have copied them down," Joe said dejectedly, "figured out the message, and met the rest of his gang."

"That means they might be digging up the treasure right now!" Chet put in.

"Let's head for Yellowknife pronto," Frank urged.

"First I'll contact Radley," said Mr Hardy.

The five exchanged hasty goodbyes with Mr Baker-Jones and took a taxi back to their hotel. Mr Hardy set up his short-wave set and radioed to his assistant. Soon they heard Sam's voice over the transmitter.

"We spotted diggers along the lake shore. Before we could apprehend them, they fled in a float plane. We found the half-buried hull of a small Viking ship. The hold was empty, but we found a few gold coins and gems. Over and out."

Frank cried excitedly, "Those crooks have found the rune stone treasure!"

"They must have used the stolen float plane we were looking for," Joe said dejectedly. "I wonder where they went."

"I'll bet they're in Wood Buffalo Park, but at another hideout."

"And they'll stay there at least until the heat's off."

"Then the gang'll try to get out of the country?" Chet asked.

"Right," said Frank. "Dad, I think we should go to Fort Smith, get camping gear, and take off into the park after the gang."

Mr Hardy agreed. "We'll leave this afternoon."

"*Bon tonnerre!*" said Caribou. "Think of all that gold!"

The group took the next flight to Fort Smith. When they arrived late that afternoon, the detectives went straight to the Hudson's Bay Company store. After buying food, picking up their gear, and hiring rifles, they went to the park administration office.

Curly Pike was there and greeted them as they entered the office. "Hi, fellows!" the pilot called out. "What are you doing back here? Still on a mystery?"

The Hardys introduced their father, then explained the proposed search. "We want to leave for Wood Buffalo Park as soon as possible," said Frank. "Could you fly us in your 'copter?"

"I sure can," Curly answered. "I'm pretty eager to

have you capture those thieves myself. Can you leave in an hour?"

Mr Hardy smiled. "I think we can, Curly. We'll meet you back here."

"I'll be ready," Curly replied.

Mr Hardy, Caribou and the boys went to a small restaurant where they had dinner. When they returned to the park office, the large helicopter was being warmed up on the field next to the administration building. Curly was at the controls and waved to his five passengers.

They climbed aboard, and seconds after the door was shut, the helicopter lifted off. Soon they were cruising over Wood Buffalo Park, and Frank, who was seated up front with Curly, directed him towards the cave where they had found the stone.

"We may as well check the spot to be sure no one is hiding there."

"I had a good look round here yesterday," Curly shouted over the roar of the rotors. "I didn't see a soul."

"We'll go farther inland to search then," Frank said.

Presently the Hardys, after conferring with Chet and Caribou, signalled for Curly to set down. When the craft landed, the boys unloaded their gear and studied maps to determine their exact location.

"Good luck," called Curly, as he boarded the helicopter. "Radio me when you want to be picked up."

"Okay," said Joe. The searchers strapped on their rucksacks and set off. Spreading out to cover the widest territory possible, they struggled and stumbled their way through thick brush and rocky, uneven terrain.

Just as it was growing dark, the group trudged across a barren hill. Reaching the top, they stood looking into a valley below. Feeding on the tall grasses was a huge herd of buffalo.

"Wow!" said Chet, when he saw the size of the hulking beasts. "They're tremendous!"

The great black animals, the boys recalled, were the true wood buffalo, not the prairie bison of the American West. On the flanks of the herd stood bulls, flicking their tails and twitching their skin to shake off the black flies.

"I read that this buffalo's skin is two inches thick," Joe said, joining his brother, "and their hair eight inches long."

"They're big," said Chet, "but they don't look very bright."

He walked ahead of his companions as they trudged downhill and skirted the edge of the herd. Chet drew near for a better look at the beasts.

"Not so close!" Caribou warned him.

Just then one of the bulls snorted and pawed the ground near the chubby boy. Suddenly the huge animal wheeled and lunged towards him.

"Yeow!" yelled Chet and stumbled backwards.

Fortunately, the bull evidently was only trying to scare off the strange human intruder. When Chet retreated, the beast rejoined his herd, keeping a wary eye on the hikers as they passed by.

"Not bright, eh?" Joe said, grinning, when Chet rejoined them.

"I take it back," Chet said, laughing.

It was dark when the group stopped to camp. The Hardys and Caribou were busy unpacking necessary gear. Suddenly Joe looked around. "Where's Chet?" he asked. The chunky boy was not in sight.

"I hope he not chase more buffalo," Caribou said, chuckling.

Just then there was a rustling in the brush and Chet stepped out. "I was just doing some exploring," he explained. "You know, it's amazing how well you can hear the robins singing in this still air."

"Wait a minute!" Frank said eagerly. "Did you say you heard robins?"

"Sure," Chet said, "as clear as a bell!"

"You couldn't have," Frank contradicted him. "There aren't any songbirds up here now. It's one of the strange things about this part of the Northwest Territories."

"That is right," Caribou agreed, puzzled. "No songbirds here in the summer."

Joe snapped his fingers. "Someone must be using the birdcall as a signal."

"*Bon tonnerre!*" Caribou muttered. "I think we get near our enemy."

"Do you think they've spotted us?" Joe asked his father.

"I'm not sure, son. But even if they have, I don't believe the gang will stop to put up a fight. They'd take the Viking treasure and run!"

"Well, let's follow *them*," Frank urged. "If they're close by, we'd better not spend extra time camping."

By now a full moon had risen and illuminated the trail chosen by the searchers. They started out in the

direction of the area where Chet had heard the "robins."
Progress was slow through the tangled underbrush.
Thorny branches tore at their clothes.

Suddenly all five stopped and listened. The sound of
men's voices came from directly ahead.

"We've located them!" Joe whispered tensely.

· 19 ·

Stampede!

"WE'VE found the thieves!" Chet repeated excitedly as the sound of voices continued.

Mr Hardy held a finger to his lips, signalled for the others to follow, and retreated a hundred feet. The boys and Caribou gathered tensely around him.

"We must make plans," he said, as they formed a huddle. "We have the element of surprise on our side."

Shielding his flashlight beam, the detective pointed it downwards and drew a large circle in the dirt.

"Caribou," said Mr Hardy, "you're the most experienced woodsman in our group. You make your way round to the far side of the spot where the men are." He indicated Caribou's position on the circle.

"*Oui*," said the French-Canadian. "I will be quiet like a mouse."

"Frank," the detective continued, "make your way to the right side, and Joe, you take the left. Chet and I will close in on the men from this direction."

Everyone slipped off his rucksack. Then Frank said, "We should be all set and ready to charge in twelve minutes."

"Better synchronize our watches," said Joe. They took his advice, as he counted off the seconds.

Caribou turned on his heels and disappeared into the forest, silently and swiftly. Just as quickly the others took off, heading for their positions. Chet and the Hardys carried rifles, and Caribou had his woodsman's knife as well.

Frank and Joe reached their respective places and ticked off the minutes. From where they crouched the boys could barely hear the voices. Tensely the Hardys waited, barely breathing.

At the appointed time, the brothers rushed forward towards the sound. But suddenly each stopped dead in his tracks.

The voices belonged to Tony and Biff!

Tony was saying, "Frank, Joe and Chet are coming to Edmonton tomorrow. Sam talked to Mr Hardy, and he said the fellows are going to search for the rune stone."

The Hardys were completely mystified. What were Tony and Biff doing here? And why was Tony repeating what had already happened?

Frank and Joe ran on until they came to a small clearing under a tree. At the same moment the others, equally mystified, converged on the spot. There was no sign of the two boys.

"Look!" Joe cried, shining his flashlight on a metal box.

"A tape recorder!" Frank exclaimed. "We heard Biff and Tony on tape!"

"A clever trick," Mr Hardy remarked wryly, as they examined the machine.

There were two packages of small batteries wired up for extra power. A spring arrangement automatically turned off the tape, rewound it, and started the player again.

"Now the crooks have really slowed us down!" Chet said disgustedly.

"Biff and Tony's room must have been bugged by some of the gang just after the fellows met Sam in Yellowknife," Joe guessed, switching off the recorder.

"Yes," Mr Hardy agreed. "From what they were saying, it was before you left Bayport."

"*Bon tonnerre!*" Caribou boomed. "Those thieves probably are far away by now."

"If they manage to reach their plane," Mr Hardy said, "we'll have a hard job stopping them."

Joe pulled out the map, and spread it on the ground. "I'd say we're at this spot," he said, pointing. "There's a lake about three miles away from here."

"Which would be a logical place for the thieves to keep their float plane," Frank added. "Maybe they haven't taken off yet."

"We'll head for the lake then," said Mr Hardy. "First, I'll radio Curly Pike and let him know where we're going."

The five headed back to the spot where they had left their equipment and in a few minutes the short-wave set was operating. Mr Hardy reached Curly on the first call, and explained what had happened. He also told Curly the route that they planned to follow.

After the detective signed off, everyone took up his gear and the party set out once again. For an hour the searchers made their way through the dense forest, travelling as quickly as possible. Just at dawn they came out of the heavy belt of trees and on to the rim of a saucer-shaped stretch of meadow, about a mile wide.

"It certainly looks peaceful," Joe commented. "No sign of the gang."

The sun began to rise, casting a rosy light across several huge boulders on the other side of the valley. The glint of water lay just beyond.

"Must be the lake," said Frank.

Exhausted from lack of sleep, the Hardys and Chet flopped down for another brief rest. Caribou paced back and forth, peering into the meadow.

"Something down there move!" he exclaimed, squinting into the faint light.

His remark brought the others to their feet. They scanned the valley intently. Among the tall grass moved a mass of dark, bulky shapes.

"Only buffalo!" Joe said in disappointment.

As the sun rose higher, the group made its descent into the meadow. They started across it, noticing that the buffalo were moving about restlessly. Some of the animals were grazing peacefully, but the bulls were snorting around the flanks of the herd.

"They probably have our scent," Frank said.

Suddenly Joe cried out. "Over there! The gang!"

On the opposite side of the valley, a group of men could be seen moving from behind one of the large boulders. They were hurrying towards the water. Suddenly one of the men wheeled round.

"They've spotted us!" Joe said grimly.

"Let's get them!" Frank broke into a run.

"Hold it!" Mr Hardy warned.

The men across the field had turned and raised their rifles.

"They're going to fire!" Chet shouted.

Three shots rang out, echoing back from the heavy boulders. A second volley followed. The next moment Caribou yelled, "They're stampeding the herd!"

No sooner had he spoken than the Hardys and their friends realized in horror that he was right. The gigantic herd of huge, shaggy buffalo had turned towards them and the beasts were pounding across the flat valley in an enormous dusty wave. The ground shook as hundreds of hoofs thundered towards the five companions. They were by now far out in the open meadow with no protective trees nearby.

"We can't get out of the way!" Joe shouted. "We'll be trampled!"

·20·

Norsemen's Treasure

THE avalanche of wild buffalo thundered on towards the Hardy group.

"Back! Run back for the trees!" Frank shouted desperately. "It's our only chance."

The five turned and raced for their lives towards the woods.

"*Ye-o-ow!*" came a yell of panic from Chet, as he tripped and fell. He lay helpless, one of the straps from his pack tangled round his leg.

Quickly Frank bent down and tugged at the strap, slipping it off. The pounding hoofs of the buffalo grew louder and nearer.

"We'll never make it, Frank!" Chet gasped, as his pal pulled him to his feet.

Suddenly there was another roar louder than that of the rampaging herd. A piercing hum split the morning air as a helicopter came across the trees and over the brow of the hill.

"*It's Curly Pike!*" Joe yelled.

The helicopter swooped down and hovered between Frank and Chet and the charging buffalo. Using his stick and rudder skilfully, the pilot brought the chopper into a half turn. The roar of the rotor blades and the thick cloud of dust they raised filled the entire area.

The dust apparently seemed like a solid wall to the charging beasts, for Frank and Chet heard the snorting animals turn to the left and thunder off in another direction.

Curly followed the buffalo as they ran, moving back and forth behind them like a sheep dog herding his flock. When he had chased the beasts to the other end of the valley, the pilot brought the helicopter back to the group and landed near them. As he jumped out, the five raced over to the aircraft, grinning with relief and gratitude.

"Thanks," Frank said, arriving first. "You came just in the nick of time!"

"I hate to think what would have happened if you hadn't!" Joe added fervently.

"Yes," Mr Hardy said, "you saved our lives."

"And how!" Chet was still shaking from the narrow escape.

"*Merci, mon ami!*" Caribou put in. "A million thanks!"

The pilot smiled. "One of the first things you learn up here is never argue with a herd of buffalo. What happened?"

Mr Hardy explained that the thieves had fired rifleshots into the herd. Then he quickly suggested a plan. "Curly, you take Frank and Joe in the 'copter and head for the lake to cut off the thieves' escape."

"Right," said the pilot. "And I'll radio to the Fort Smith Mounties for reinforcements."

Caribou and Chet, too, were eager for action. "What's our next move, Mr Hardy?" Chet asked.

"We'll track the gang on foot," the detective replied.

"If they backtrack, we may be able to capture them."

The two teams quickly departed on their separate missions. As Mr Hardy, with Chet and Caribou, moved swiftly across the valley, the helicopter lifted Frank, Joe and Curly into the air.

"Let's make straight for that lake," Frank urged. The pilot complied, then radioed the RCMP station, which promised help at once.

A few minutes later the helicopter was hovering over the quiet water. "Look below!" Joe exclaimed. "A float plane! Must be the gang's stolen one!"

Tensely the Hardys and Curly scanned the surrounding area for any sign of the enemy. They could see no-one. "We'd better hurry and fix their plane so they can't escape in it," Frank said. "Suppose I go down and fasten a rope to the plane so that we can tow it away."

"Good idea," Curly agreed. "The Mounties might not get here before the crooks do."

He kept the chopper about thirty feet above the water while Frank snapped the lowering harness under his arms. Joe then fastened a hook at the end of the descent wire to the ring in the middle of the harness, and gave a sharp tug to make sure it was secure.

"All set!" Frank said tersely.

Soon Joe was carefully turning the winch and letting his brother down to the float plane. Frank dropped into position on its left pontoon. He unsnapped the hook from his harness and made three quick turns with the cable round one of the float's struts.

He looked up at Curly and signalled. The pilot eased the helicopter forward. While Frank kept a firm grip on the strut, the float plane was towed rapidly across the water.

"That's great," said Joe.

Curly built up speed and the plane skimmed towards shore. At the right moment, Frank released the half hitch on the strut and the craft's momentum carried it upon to the beach among the trees.

The young sleuth hopped off the pontoon and ran along the shore. He stopped beneath the hovering helicopter and grabbed the lifting wire which dangled from it. In a moment he was being hauled up by the winch.

When he was aboard once more, Joe praised his brother. "Nice going!" As the helicopter gained altitude and headed towards the centre of the lake, Joe added, "And not a second too soon! Look!"

The trio spotted a group of men, armed with rifles, standing on the far shore. They were gesticulating frantically and pointing to the spot where they had left the float plane. "The gang!" Frank exclaimed.

Suddenly the thieves caught sight of the helicopter as it swooped towards them.

"Hey! Kelly's there!" Joe cried out as he recognized the pale, thin man. The next moment the outlaws broke and ran for the shelter of the trees.

"They're heading into the forest!" Frank said.

"It won't do them much good," Curly said, pointing. "Your father, Caribou and Chet are closing in from that side."

"They sure are!" Joe said, as he intently watched the three familiar figures encircle the thieves.

Just then those in the helicopter saw three float

planes swoop low over the lake. One after another, they splashed on to the surface and taxied towards the beach.

"The Mounties!" Joe yelled. "We really have the gang trapped!"

Curly dropped the helicopter over the sandy beach and set down near the RCMP planes. He and the Hardys hopped out and ran to where Corporal Fergus and his men were snapping handcuffs on the four surly-looking gangsters. Mr Hardy and the others came up at the same time.

"No escape this time, Kelly," the corporal was saying to the prisoner.

"Where's the treasure from the Viking ship?" Frank shot the question at the captured thieves.

Kelly glared at him, but indicated three canvas sacks lying near the rifles and packs. "Over there," he said in a sullen voice.

Mr Hardy, Caribou and the boys ran eagerly to the bags and opened them rapidly. Reaching deep into a sack, Chet pulled out a handful of glittering gold coins.

"Wow! Look at these!" he cried.

"And this statue must be worth a fortune!" Frank held up the gold figure of a Viking warrior.

"This is a historical find, as well as a valuable one," Mr Hardy said. "It definitely links the exploration of northern Canada to the ancient Norsemen."

The other three prisoners—Mike, Red, and Fats— were Americans. Fats was the pilot who had made off with the float plane on Great Slave Lake. They were eager to talk, and named Kelly and Dulac as the instigators of all the robberies.

They disclosed that Kelly was his real name, although

he sometimes used the alias Jesse Keating. He was the ringleader. A disbarred lawyer from northern Maine, Kelly once had been associated with a law firm in Quebec, where he had handled a case which involved the history of Vikings and rune stones. A Canadian museum was suing a man who had sold a rune stone, which later proved to be a hoax.

While delving into rune stone history, Kelly had uncovered a fragmentary clue to the whereabouts of a treasure buried on the shore of Great Slave Lake by Vikings who had explored inland for hundreds of miles. Thinking that Great Slave Lake was part of an ocean, they had stopped to construct a sturdy ship, only to find that the body of water was a vast lake.

This information had started Kelly on the quest of the treasure, and when he learned of the find which Caron had made, Kelly figured it might contain more specific information about the treasure. His guess had proved to be astute.

But Kelly had been dismayed when he learned through a London confederate that the famous Fenton Hardy had been called in on the case. The Bayport venture was to frighten him off, if possible, and to glean more information about rune stones from the excellent collection of reference books in Bayport Library.

"So you wrecked our short-wave antenna," Joe said to Kelly.

The prisoner confessed nothing, but gave him a baleful stare.

"Who *actually* stole the stone and money?" Mr Hardy asked the handcuffed men.

"Dulac and Kelly!" the man named Fats answered

readily. "That was a real mistake, because then Caribou was squarely on your side after they grabbed his two thousand bucks."

"Who tossed that knife at me in Fort Smith, and caused our canoe to leak on Slave River?" Frank demanded of Red.

The grizzled prisoner replied that Dulac had been responsible for both acts. Red also confessed to having driven the getaway car for Kelly in Bayport.

Upon their return to Canada, they had contacted the rest of the gang and assigned Dulac to trail and harass the Hardy boys.

"*Bon tonnerre!*" Caribou exploded. "I knew that trap-robbin' weasel was no good!"

After further questioning, the Hardys learned that the lodge thefts around Great Slave Lake were continued partly to finance Kelly's venture. The remainder of Caribou's money, fifteen hundred dollars, was found and returned to him. The Bayport Library book, stolen by Kelly, had been picked up by Fats, who handed it over. Mike had posed as Fenton Hardy.

As for the mysterious radio threat picked up in Bayport, that was Red's doing, he confessed. "We had hoped to scare off Hardy by threats and sabotage," he grumbled. "But it didn't work."

"You can say that again," Chet chirped.

Corporal Fergus and his men put the four thieves into the RCMP float planes for the trip back to Fort Smith. The Mountie shook hands with the Hardys and their friends.

"Congratulations!" he said. "You solved a tough case."

"Thanks to my sons and their buddies," the detective replied.

The Hardys, Chet, and Caribou boarded the Wood Buffalo Park helicopter, with Curly at the controls. They were all in high spirits as Frank radioed Radley in Yellowknife and told him the good news. The two groups would meet that night at Fort Smith.

On the way back, Curly set the helicopter down near one of the buffalo which had been shot by the gang. Adeptly the pilot skinned one of the beasts.

"What are you going to do with the meat?" Joe asked.

"Most of this goes to the Indians," Curly answered, grinning at Chet's dubious look. "Buffalo's fine eating. I'll save a big roast for your supper tonight."

A few hours later at Fort Smith a joyous reunion took place when Radley, Biff and Tony arrived at the hotel.

"You fellows are first-rate detectives," Biff said, congratulating the Hardys and Chet.

"And we've learned a real lesson," Tony said. "We'll never let anybody eavesdrop on us again."

"You can say that again!" Biff added earnestly.

Mr Hardy smiled. "What counts is you've both learned a valuable lesson in sleuthing, done your part to help solve the case, and earned the bonus."

"We're all ready for another mystery," said Biff with a grin.

"But no stampedes, please," Chet added.

The Hardy boys' next case was along completely different lines. They called it *The Mystery of the Chinese Junk*.

"Let's celebrate the Viking symbol mystery by

having dinner!" Joe urged. "That bison roast might taste pretty good."

"It should be ready by now," Frank said. "Curly gave it to the cook when he got back."

The group was seated around the table when a waiter entered carrying a huge platter with a gigantic buffalo roast.

"*Bon tonnerre!*" Chet said with a grin. "Look at the size of that! Enough for twenty Vikings!"

"And for Chet Morton, too!" Joe joked.

Everyone laughed, then Caribou lifted a carving knife. "*Mes amis,*" he said, "this feast is most happy farewell."

The Hardy Boys® Mystery Stories
by Franklin W. Dixon

There are many exciting Hardy Boys Mysteries in Armada. Have you read these?

The Clue of the Screeching Owl (9)

A terrifying apparition haunts gloomy Black Hollow. Camping in the woods, the Hardy Boys face spinechilling danger . . .

Hunting for Hidden Gold (25)

Frank and Joe go to the Wild West in search of treasure. But a deadly trap awaits them among the abandoned gold mines . . .

The Outlaw's Silver (65)

The Hardys face one of their trickiest missions — to destroy a vicious spy ring. But first they must cross miles and miles of unknown, treacherous forest . . .

The Four-Headed Dragon (67)

What is the link between an eerie old mansion and a plan to sabotage an oil pipeline? Only the Hardy Boys can find out in time . . .

Armada

The Nancy Drew Mystery Stories®
by Carolyn Keene

Have you read all the titles in this thrilling series?

The Quest of the Missing Map (6)

Nancy's search for buried treasure takes her to exotic Little Palm Island. But someone is desperate to find the hoard before her . . .

The Ghost of Blackwood Hall (11)

Blood-curdling danger awaits Nancy when she investigates a mansion haunted by a terrifying phantom . . .

The Swami's Ring (55)

Eastern mysticism and mystery go hand in hand for Nancy when she searches for a stolen ring — fabulous jewel of the maharajahs. But deep in the woods a deadly snake lies in wait for her . . .

The Twin Dilemma (57)

When a glamorous New York model disappears, Nancy steps in to take her place. But the glittering world of fashion hides an ugly secret . . .

Armada

SUPERSLEUTHS

by FRANKLIN W. DIXON and CAROLYN KEENE

A feast of reading for all mystery fans!

At last, the Hardy Boys and Nancy Drew have joined forces to become the world's most brilliant detective team!

Together, the daredevil sleuths investigate seven spine-chilling mysteries: a deadly roller-coaster that hurtles to disaster, a sinister bell that tolls in a city of skeletons, a haunted opera house with a sinister curse — and many more terrifying situations.

Nancy Drew and the Hardy Boys — *dynamite!*

Armada

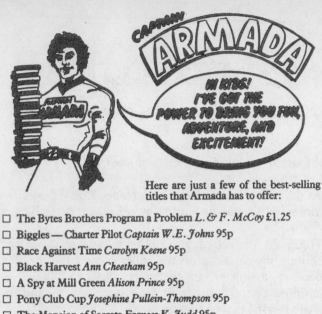